THE ALIEN'S WINGS

GRACE KENSINGTON

1

————

"I found it."

Lynx tossed the broken piece of the ship that he held in his hand back to the ground and started back across the room toward Rain. She was crouched in the wreckage with her back to him but he could see that she was holding something in her lap. The room around them was in remarkable condition compared to the rest of the ravaged ship. Though it was still crushed and broken, much of the room was still standing and appeared almost as Lynx assumed it did when the ship was in service. This had been the private quarters of the captain of the ship that had brought the Nyx 23 crew to Uoria, and out of respect they had left it as it was after the crash rather than breaking it down to make into the buildings of their settlement as they had with the rest of the ship.

Rain turned around and showed Lynx the box that she held on her thighs. She looked like she was almost cradling the box as she looked up at him with difficult to decipher emotion in her eyes. He felt a deep, painful pull in his chest as he looked at her. He had known that she was different since the moment that he met her, that she had been locked in place by the vicious and vengeful Covra and had been lying in place for more than a century. Knowing this, however, didn't change how it made him feel when he looked at her and saw those years reflected back at him through her eyes. It was in that moment that he could really feel the differences in the lives that they had lived and realized just how distanced their realities were from one another. No matter how deeply the two of them loved each other and how much they truly wanted to be together, there was no arguing the reality that they would never completely and fully understand each other. What she had gone through in the decades before he was even born was something that he could never fathom, and it would be his struggle for the rest of their lives to not only do everything that he could to understand as much of her as possible, but also to show her that even if he didn't completely understand her, he still loved her fully, totally, and without reservation.

Lynx approached her carefully and lowered himself down onto the ground with her. She continued to hold the box reverently and he wondered what emotions were moving through her in that moment. After she shared the horrifying memories of finding the captain dead moments before the crash Lynx knew that there was much more to this experience than he had originally thought and he was determined to help her get through it in whatever way that would soothe the ache within her.

"Do you want to open it?" he asked after several long moments.

"I don't know," Rain said back softly. She looked down at the box and ran her hand along it. "What do you think that I'm going to find in here?" she asked, looking up at him.

"I don't know," he said, shaking his head. "I don't know what would be in there. I'm still not completely sure what it is."

Rain nodded as if what he had said was undeniable truth and glanced back down at the box.

"What if what we find in here is horrible? What if it tells me something that I really don't want to know?"

"What could you find out that would be so horrible?" Lynx asked. "What could be in there that would be something so terrible you just don't want to know?"

She looked up at him and he could see the thoughts churning in her eyes. He hoped that asking her that would give her the confidence to open the box that she had been so aggressively searching for and let her know that no matter what was inside, she would be able to handle it.

"What if the captain was involved in all of this?" she asked. "We always assumed that having our travel course manipulated so that we came to Uoria and crashed was completely the work of the Valdicians and that there was nothing that anyone on the ship could do about it. What if that wasn't the case at all? Maybe the captain actually knew about the prison colony on Penthos and created the entire Nyx 23 project as a ruse to get scientists up here so that the Validicians could use them as they pleased. Maybe he knew that they were allies with the Covra here and were looking for a powerful species to act as their slaves and help them with their mission to take over the planet and ultimately the rest of the galaxy so he created this entire project under the guise that it was about freeing the planet and saving everyone on it, when in reality he knew all the time that we were going to end up on Uoria."

It was a possibility that Lynx hadn't considered, and one that made him feel like there was ice water running through his veins. The thought that the captain, the man that the rest of the crew trusted above all others and without reservation, would have actually be one to betray them was something that Lynx couldn't fathom. Even when Pyra had been so cruel in the settlement and imprisoned the Mikana men, he had done it thinking that what he was doing was the right thing to protect his kind and guard the future for his son. He would never had given up the life, safety, and comfort of the Denynso for someone else. Lynx couldn't even imagine the level of pain and betrayal that that kind of revelation would have caused him and the other warriors.

"You said that he was dead when you found him," Lynx said cautiously. She hadn't yet said the actual words that the captain was dead when she discovered him in his control room right before the crash, but she knew and he had to force her to think about it so that she could understand. "What do you think killed him?"

Rain didn't look at him. She continued to run her palm along the box and suddenly let out a breath. She didn't respond to his question, but he knew that she was thinking about it. Finally she took the latch on the front of the box with a shaky hand and released it. Designed specifically to withstand a disaster, the box was unharmed and only small vines that had grown up around it indicated that it had been sitting among the wreckage for more than 100 years. The lid opened without resistance and fell back to reveal its contents.

Rain lowered the box to the ground and began to sift through the items inside. Nothing that Lynx saw had any meaning for him, but Rain touched each of them carefully and with respect. Even with her concerns about the pilot possibly betraying all of them, she still felt incredible loyalty to the man who had led then in their mission and who they had thought of and memorialized in everything that they had done on Uoria since the crash. Suddenly she moved aside a piece of paper and Lynx saw a small book sitting on the bottom of the box. It was bound in dark leather and a name was embossed in gold across the front.

"Etan," he read.

"That was the pilot's name," she explained.

She touched the name with her fingertips. There was no romance in the touch, just a deep sense of connection that reached the memories within her that she had until recently refused to allow herself to speak. Lynx knew that she had spent her time in the settlement trying to overcome what she had found in the pilot's control room before the crash, and never sharing it with anyone. Greyson had been there just a few moments after the crash and given her the light that confirmed that she was looking at the body of the pilot. She had never told him, though, that she was sure that Etan had been dead for some time before the crash. She had never told any of the crew what she thought had happened to him or what that meant for the rest of the team.

Rain opened the book and scanned a few of the pages. Lynx leaned closer so that he could look at the pages along with her. Each page was filled with close, tight handwriting that seemed to chronicle what the pilot was going through each day.

"What is this?" he asked Rain.

She turned the page and started reading the next set of tiny handwriting.

"It's his journal," she explained. "It's a book that people use to record what is happening in their lives and what they are feeling. Do the Denynso do that?"

Lynx shook his head.

"No," he said. "What does it say?"

"He recorded the entire mission from a few days before we left. He talks about what he was thinking about our goals in the quest and what he was hoping to get out of it."

"So he wasn't an ally of the Validicians."

Rain nodded, letting out a breath that sounded calm and relieved.

"I don't think so. This was his private journal. He never intended on anyone else reading it. He would have no reason to conceal what he was thinking or how he was feeling about his actual motivations if they weren't what we thought they were going to be."

"That's good," Lynx said. "Right?"

He felt strangely out of control in the situation. He wanted to comfort and support her, but it was like he was looking at her from the other side of all of the time that had passed since that moment when she crouched beside the pilot's body and realized that he was dead. Rather than being there with her and looking back through those moments alongside her, he felt as though she had somehow transported back to that moment and he was now separated from her in a way that he couldn't overcome on his own. He would have to wait for her to come back to him.

Rain nodded again and continued through the book. As the pages progressed Lynx realized that the handwriting was getting larger and more erratic. Some pages only had a few words while others were so full it was almost impossible for them to read them properly. She was growing close to the pages that would describe their arrival on the planet that held the illegal prison colony, a planet that would later come to be known as Penthos, when a sheet of paper slipped out from between the pages and fluttered onto the ground between them. Rain reached down slowly and picked it up. Lynx watched her stare at the folded paper for a few moments, her eyes looking as though she were nervous to open it.

Finally she lowered the journal to her legs and used both trembling hands to carefully open the fold and smooth the paper out so that they could read it.

"What is it?" Lynx asked.

"I don't know," Rain said softly.

She turned the paper around in her hands and continued to stare at the faint image.

"It looks like a map," Lynx said, reaching forward to run his finger along one of the lines that appeared to be a road.

"A map to what?" Rain asked.

Lynx took the paper from her hands and looked down at it, trying to decipher the symbols and shapes on the map. Something about the map looked strangely familiar. He continued to stare at it, turning it in his hands so that he looked at it from different angles as the memory that was lingering in the back of his mind continued to come to shape and deepen so that he could examine it further. Finally the memory came to the front of his mind and he realized that he was looking at a map that looked very much like the one that the Denynso warriors had discovered in the prison that had led them to the Nyx 23 settlement during their first exploration of the planet.

"I think it is Uoria," he said. "It looks like a primitive sketching of the planet." He touched an area toward the top corner. "This is where the Denynso compound is. This," he gestured toward another area of the map further down and to one side, "is where your settlement was built."

Rain reached over and took the map from his hands and gazed down at it. She touched her fingertips to the area of the map where he had said the settlement was found and ran them along toward the center of the paper.

"Then this is about where we crashed."

"What does that mean?" Lynx asked, pointing toward a symbol on the top corner opposite of the Denysno compound.

Rain shook her head.

"I don't know. Do you know what is in that area of Uoria?"

"No," he said. "Remember when we left the compound and came to your settlement was the first time that we had left the compound. I don't know of anything that is on Uoria except for what I have seen since then."

Rain looked at the map again and gestured toward another area of the planet.

"This is where the Mikana kingdom is," she told him.

"Why would the pilot have a map of Uoria in his journal?" Lynx asked. "I thought that you said that you didn't even know that the planet existed."

"We didn't," Rain said. "At least, I didn't. The rest of the project crew said that they didn't either. We had never come across it in our preparation for the mission. That was why when we crashed we didn't know where we were or what to do. It was a foreign planet to us and we didn't even have any context of what the planet might be like. It made building our settlement and learning what we could eat much more challenging than it would have been if we had known anything about this planet."

"If he didn't know that the planet existed, though, how would Etan have a map of it? What would he use it for if he didn't know what it was?"

Rain picked up the journal again and Lynx could see her eyes roaming rapidly across the pages, taking in the words as quickly as she could. She turned the pages harshly the further she read and he could see color creeping across her cheeks.

"He knew," she said, her voice now low and gravelly with anger.

"What do you mean he knew? What did he know?" Lynx asked.

"He knew that Uoria was here. He knew that we were coming here."

"I don't understand," he said.

Rain shook her head.

"*I hope that what I have discovered is not true,*" she read. "*In our time in the prison colony I was able to breach the inner quarters of one of the Valdician officers. In it I found what I believed to be the personal journal of the officer. I stole a map that I found in it. I didn't have the time to read everything that the journal entry said, but it led me to believe that the Valdicians anticipated our arrival. They do not intend on allowing us to go back to Earth. This map is to a planet that they call Uoria and I fear that they are planning to send us there. I don't know why they would want us on this planet or what awaits us there if we allow them to send us there, but I can only hope that if I am not able to overcome them that having this map will help me to lead my crew even there.*"

"How did the Valdicians know that you were coming?" Lynx asked.

"There must have been a leak. Someone on our crew must have betrayed us."

"But why didn't he tell the rest of you when you got back on the ship and left the planet with the prison colony? Wouldn't he think that all of you deserved to know what was going on?"

Rain turned the page and scanned the entry.

"The ship is no longer under my command. I am terrified and do not know what to do. The rest of the team doesn't know and I am doing everything that I can to keep them from finding out. They believe that I am still piloting this ship and that we are on the proper course back to Earth. I do not know how much longer I will be able to conceal from them that the weapons the Valdicians attached to our ship have taken over our internal control system and are now bringing the ship off course and in what I can only assume is the direction of this planet Uoria. What will I tell them? How will I confess to them that I have guided them toward a fate that could be more horrible than any of us can fathom?" She let out a breath and looked at Lynx. "He wanted to protect us."

"Is there anything else?"

Rain turned the page and Lynx saw that the handwriting had returned to the tight, controlled hand of the earlier entries as if the pilot had stepped back from the panic that had taken over his mind and was now able to think clearly again. The precision in the shape of the words showed a man who had pushed away fear and was now looking ahead with clarity and determination. Lynx could hear the tears in Rain's voice as she read the entry.

"I had hoped desperately that I would be able to find a way to reclaim the ship under my own control and prevent it from going to Uoria. That hope is now lost. The technology that the Valdicians have used to take over the ship is beyond anything that I have ever seen and I cannot even begin to decipher it. It has not just taken over the control of the ship, but has also destroyed all forms of communication. We are not able to access any one in our mission control team or any of the other ships that are traveling through the galaxy. We are completely alone and there is nothing that we can do. I know now that we will never return to Earth. Never again will we see the planet that we have called home or the people who we love. I wish that there was more than

I could do for the people who have followed me with such devotion and determination. I believe that the map that I found shows where the Valdicians intend for us to be when we find our way to Uoria. I can only imagine what horrors may await us there, if we even survive our arrival. I have decided that I am not going to tell the crew what I know. They already know that the ship is no longer under our control and that we have moved completely off course. I know that telling them about the map and what I think about the Validicians will only cause them to panic and ruin what morale we have left. There is no reason to do that to them. They followed me, Journal. They trusted me. I am responsible for what has happened to us. As I lead them toward death I know that it should be me that leads them into death. I can only pray for all of our souls and that one day someone will understand."

The tears were streaming down Rain's face by the time that she finished. She turned the page of the journal but all of the papers that followed were blank. Lynx rested his hand on her back and she turned to look at him.

"He killed himself," she whispered. "He felt so guilty because he thought that he was responsible for all of this and didn't believe that we would survive. He believed that he should be the first of us to die."

"I'm so sorry," Lynx said.

He knew that it wasn't enough. There wasn't anything that he would be able to say that would be enough in this situation, and those words were the only ones that he was able to bring forward. He wished that he could do something, anything, to ease the pain that he knew that his mate was feeling, and take away the guilt and the suffering that he could see crossing her face. Rain continued to look into his eyes for several more seconds and then he saw a sudden spark of light in them as if a thought had come into her mind.

"The map," she said.

He reached for it and handed it to her.

"What about it?" he asked.

Rain spread the map out over the journal and ran her hand across it.

"You said that this would be where the Denynso compound is," she said, gesturing to the area on the map that Lynx had showed her.

"That's right," Lynx said.

"And this would be where the settlement that we made is," she said, gesturing to that area of the map.

"Yes," Lynx told her. "And this is the wreckage," he said, pointing to the area of the map that was approximately where they were as they crouched among the final remnants of the ship ruins.

"Then what is this?" Rain asked, touching her fingertip to the symbol toward the opposite corner of the Denynso compound.

Lynx looked at it and shook his head.

"I don't know what's up there."

"Neither do I," Rain said. "And maybe that's the point."

"What do you mean?"

"This is the map that Etan found in the Validician officer's quarters, right?"

"Yes," Lynx said, narrowing his eyes as he focused in on Rain's rapidly increasing pace.

"If he took this map directly from the journal that it was in and put it in his journal that means that that symbol was drawn by the Validician officer. Now, Etan didn't say in his journal exactly what he read in that book, but he said that he knew the Validicians knew we were coming and they planned on sending us to Uoria. That means that there was a plan all along. It wasn't something that just suddenly came to the Validicians when we showed up."

"Which means that this symbol is part of the plan," Lynx said.

"Exactly," Rain replied, the tears now dry in her eyes as she looked at him. "But what if the plan didn't turn out the way that it was supposed to?"

"What do you mean?"

"The Validicians obviously had this planned out. We know now that they had an alliance with the Covra and that they sent us here as an offering to them. The Covra wanted to take over the planet and then the rest of the galaxy."

"Etan didn't know that, though," Lynx said.

"No, he didn't. But he did know that they knew that we were coming here, and if they knew that we were coming here, they had a plan for where we were going to end up."

Lynx looked down at the map again and his eyes locked on the symbol. Realization hit him and he felt his heartrate increase.

"You crashed in the wrong place," he said.

Rain nodded.

"All along they intended us to crash somewhere closer to whatever this symbol indicates. This is where the Covra expected us to be, and we didn't end up there. Instead, we crashed here and made our settlement on the other side of the planet. That's why it took so long for the Covra to find us and start their attacks. They thought that we were going to be in a completely different place."

"But what place?" Lynx asked. "What is in this area of the planet that made them choose this place specifically?"

"A Covra compound?" Rain asked.

"I don't think so," Lynx said. "Remember what we found out about the Covra. They can't build anything on their own. They have to use the power of other creatures to do anything. I doubt that they have any type of settlement or compound or anything that would be so obvious or extensive. They need to be able to move around easily and undetectably so that they can find other creatures to manipulate and to use as incubators."

"But the Validicians were the allies of the Covra. Wouldn't they want us to crash near them?"

"Not necessarily," Lynx said. "They were sending the Covra a group that they knew were going to be powerful tools in their mission to take over. You were here for 15 years before the Covra laid their eggs. That means that you weren't brought here just to be their incubators. It wouldn't make sense for the Validicians to send a group to the planet so long before the Covra would be ready to reproduce. You were sent here for another reason. Where they intended you to crash had something to do with that original intent. Wherever this place is," he said, pointing at the symbol, "it was where you were originally supposed to go and where the Covra thought they would find you. That means there is something there that had something to do with their goal of taking over the planet. Something that might have much more extensive impact than we know."

"We need to find out what is there," Rain said. "If we're right and the Validicians had this planned before we even got to Penthos, there was much more going on than just that. There could still be danger. Even after all this time, there could still be something there that could put Uoria and everyone on it at risk. We need to get back to the settlement and pack as many supplies as we can. We need to get there as fast as possible."

Lynx nodded and helped Rain to her feet as she put everything back in the box and tucked it under her arm to carry back to the settlement with her. He knew that there was a journey ahead of them that could be long and dangerous, but he would walk beside her and give her all of the strength and courage that he had within him. This was unlike any battle that he had ever faced and he knew that he would fight harder for her than he had ever fought.

2

———

They walked along the edge of the badlands, away from the flames that licked up toward the sky, but Maxim could still feel the heat of the burning compound beneath his feet. With every step he was reminded of the destruction that his ancestors had caused to this area of the planet. It hurt him to think of the pain that they had caused, the suffering that they had doled out to the Denynso who had once called this area of Uoria their home. He remembered what Creia had told them about the badlands and how they had come to be, but in his heart he felt that there was more to it than just what the king had said.

"What do you remember about the badlands, Athan?" he asked, turning toward the older man.

He could see in Athan's eyes that being in this area was painful for him and that the memories brewing within him were ones that he thought he would never have to face again.

"They weren't the badlands then," Athan told him, his voice slipping away into memory as he spoke. "This area of

Uoria was more beautiful than anything that exists today. It was lush and fertile. This is where the belief that the sunrises of the Denynso compound were the most incredible that existed and that the warriors gained their strength and courage from the light of those sunrises originated. There had already been extensive conflict here. Those who had divided from the kingdom had already come seeking alliances with the Denynso."

"This was before the Order became corrupted," Maxim said.

"Yes," Athan confirmed. "The first to split from the kingdom did so after the tragedies with the Covra. They broke away and traveled to Ynn, only to return later and continue with renewed efforts to take over Uoria. That is when the Order began to change."

"The Covra had already been here," Maxim told him. "Creia told us that the Covra and the Validicians had both come to this compound generations before to find alliances and the Denynso rejected them."

"That is when the Covra found out about us," Athan said. "There was no darkness or corruption or greed in our kind then. There was only gentleness and peace. We had good relations with the Denynso of this compound and some even cooperated with those of the other compounds."

"Creia told us that those clans disappeared and that no one knows what happened to them."

"That's right," Athan said. "They were not as friendly as the clan that lived here, but they still cooperated with us. I am convinced that when the Covra found that they wouldn't be able to align with the Denynso that they decided to enslave them, just as they wanted to do with the other species so that they could work toward taking over this planet and the others throughout the galaxy. In order to do that, though, they first needed to build up their army. Together with the Valdicians they went after the species that would not expect them and that could fulfill the work that they needed done. They came after us. It was that decision that many years later led to our kingdom dividing and the greed, avarice, and cruelty to build in those who left. That is the first time that the Order fought the Klimnu. That was when the Denynso divided and half left this compound to create the compound that is there now."

"Did they know what they were then?" Maxim asked.

"Of course," Athan answered. "Just like you said before we came here, their appearance hadn't changed at all yet. They wouldn't for more than 250 years. They left Uoria just as beautiful as they were when they left the kingdom. The Order aligned with the Denynso to combat the group and force them off of the planet, hoping that if they were to go somewhere else they would soon lose the viciousness that formed in them because of the torment our kind went through. The Order hoped that the time away would restore their kindness and purity of spirit so that they could return and reunite with the rest of the kingdom."

"That didn't happen," Maxim said. "It only got worse."

"Yes," Athan said. "Their time away from the planet only intensified the change that they had already gone through. Not their physical change. Remember that still hadn't happened. It was the change within them that was the worst of the transformations that came over them. Being away from Uoria and the connection with the rest of the kingdom took away the reminders of beauty, love, and perseverance that kept the rest of the kingdom going even through the darkness. As new generations were born they weren't taught about what had happened to the Mikana to turn their hearts cold. Instead, they only learned hatred and it was that hatred that would push the planet toward destruction. When they returned from Ynn, they went right back to where it had all begun and tried again to get the cooperation of the Denynso, hoping that over the time that they had spent off of the planet that the other species would have been successful in changing how they felt. Of course, you know that it didn't work that way."

"The Denynso on this compound didn't want anything to do with the Klimnu and told them to leave again."

"Exactly," Athan said. "They still remembered the invasions of the Covra, Valdicians, and Klimnu from years before. By then the memories of the Order had faded and only the fear of the Klimnu lingered. They told the Klimnu that they wanted nothing to do with them and that they needed to leave. This infuriated the group, a group that didn't even remember that the Mikana existed or that their kind had once been a part of a kingdom here on Uoria. These were creatures who believed that they had originated on Ynn and that they were the only ones of their kind in any form. I know in my heart that it was that belief that saved the rest of the kingdom."

"You think that if they remembered the Mikana that they would have come back and destroyed us?" Maxim asked.

"Absolutely," Athan said. "They would have wanted to kill off those who they felt were a betrayal because they didn't choose to let the darkness take over them."

"Instead they destroyed this compound."

"The Denynso refused to be their allies and help them to explore other planets and seek out slaves."

"Just like the Covra wanted to."

"Yes. And when they did that, the Klimnu were infuriated. All of the anger and pain that had built within them from all of the generations of Klimnu who had lived on Ynn poured out and they not only destroyed this compound but ensured that it would burn forever. They transformed what was incredibly beautiful into what we know as the badlands."

"But you saw it before they destroyed it."

"Oh, yes. The Order tried to stop the Klimnu from causing any trouble with the Denynso or with any other species. We confronted them and fought against them. We formed alliances with the other species that I told you about. We walked into battle against them several times. We didn't know then that each time we confronted them, the corruption within our very own was getting worse. It wasn't long before the members of the Order had started to change. Aegeus knew it. He knew something was going to happen. It was after that final battle, after he died, that the Klimnu destroyed the compound. It was as if his determination to protect Uoria and resolve what had happened within the Order had been what protected it. When he died, the Klimnu, both the outsider group and those within the Order itself, were able to rise up and destroy the compound. I watched it burn, knowing that with it burned all hope that Aegeus's plans would ever be fulfilled."

"The weapons," Ivy suddenly said.

Maxim turned to her and saw that her eyes were wide and her mouth slightly parted.

"What?" he asked.

"The weapons," she repeated. "Remember when Rain was telling us about how Nyx 23 ended up here? She talked about the weapons that the Valdicians used. They were able to control them with their minds, but some of them also threw them. They were powerful enough to destroy the inner workings of their ship."

"That is what the Klimnu used to detonate the volcanoes," Maxim said, realization settling over him. "How did they get them?"

Athan shook his head.

"I don't know," he said.

"What happened after the battle?" Maxim asked.

"I went back to the kingdom," Athan said. "I had to tell your mother..."

"No," Maxim said. "I know that. What happened to the Order? What happened to the members who were Klimnu?"

"Most left and joined with them. No one knows where they went or what they did, but within two years they had come into contact with those flowers and started their physical transformations. Some came back to the kingdom, but were so gruesome that they were sent away. Some were killed. The others remained with the Klimnu group and went with them to Creia to implore him to heal them."

Maxim shuddered at the horrific details and shook his head.

"I don't understand. Why would they go to Creia? They had just destroyed the compound where the clan had once lived only two years before."

"But it had been generations since the clan had split. Yes, Creia and many of the others had spent their childhoods going back and forth between the compounds to stay connected with the descendants of family who had remained in the original compound and there were many who felt that it was truly just one large compound now that they thought that the threat of the Klimnu was gone, but it was still a divided clan. They hoped to appeal to the honor of the Denynso, especially one who was both warrior and healer."

"I never knew that Creia was a healer," Nylek said.

He had remained silent throughout the entire journey

and it startled Maxim slightly to hear the voice of the warrior who he had nearly forgotten was accompanying them. Maxim remembered that this young warrior was not one of the men who had been a part of the group that had left the compound and had likely not heard everything that Creia had told them.

"You didn't know that the Klimnu asked him to heal them and he sent them away?" Maxim asked.

"When Leia told us about her time in the prison with the Klimnu she said that the Klimnu who tormented her the most told her that they had asked Creia for help, that they knew that he would be able to heal them. I didn't realize that meant that he was an actual healer."

Athan nodded.

"Creia is a Denynso of truly unbelievable power. He is the source of virtually all of the myths and legends that other species hear about your kind. In the Mikana kingdom it has been so long since there was any cooperation between our kind and the Denynso that the thoughts of the species had turned mostly to legend. Many of our young people did not even believe that the Denynso warriors really existed until Pyra and his men came into the kingdom. I suppose it is just like none of the young generations of the Denynso knowing that the Klimnu originated as Mikana. Time tends to blur lines and erase details until people aren't sure what to believe anymore. It takes away the truth and changes it until it is almost unrecognizable."

Maxim felt like he had been knocked off balance by everything that he had just heard. It seemed that every time that he thought that he was on the right path toward understanding what had happened or even just the origins of the different species that inhabited the planet, he learned something that made him question what he thought that he already knew.

Athan's description of the fire that had destroyed the compound and turned it into the badlands still rolling through his mind, Maxim turned to stare at the still-burning ground of the badlands. In the glow of the flames breaking through the dark ground and sending sparks up against the black night sky he could almost see the lingering presence of the men who had lost their lives there. Among the shadowy images of those who had fought so hard to protect it but were cut down and tossed aside he could see his father. He knew that Aegeus had walked on this ground, left his footsteps on the dirt that now burned. The thought of the ground where his father had lived, fought, died, and lain now engulfed by flames was almost too painful for Maxim to contemplate. He longed to know where his father had stood when he was cut down so that he could stand there and be more connected to the man who he had missed for so long. Even more now he ached to understand what had happened to Aegeus's body after he had died. It still didn't make any sense that he had simply disappeared. Especially now that Maxim knew that he had walked into the battle carrying the sword that his father had carried, he couldn't rationalize in his mind how his father's body and his grandfather's massive sword could just vanish without any trace leftover for Athan to find and bring home to them.

Now more than ever Maxim believed that there was far more to those last moments of his father's existence than he knew, and likely far more than even Athan knew. Part of him had wanted to distrust Athan. Despite him being so important to the family throughout his entire life, the older man had been the only link that Maxim had to the moment of his father's death. Even though that could have made him even more precious, in Maxim's mind it made him, in a way, a threat. Rather than feeling the connection and being grateful that at least Aegeus had had Athan with him until the end, Maxim felt suspicious of Athan and the information that he had shared with them from the time that Maxim and Kyven were children. He believed that there was more for Athan to tell him, and felt embittered by the fact that the older man seemed completely reluctant to share it. Faced with the reality of the burning badlands, though, the realization that Athan was the only one of the kingdom outside of his family who he could trust. He knew now that Athan had truly told him everything that he could and that if there was anything else that he hadn't told them, it was because he didn't know that the information mattered.

They had been roaming the edge of the badlands for long enough that the horizon had gone from inky blackness to a soft pink as the sun started to rise. Maxim remembered his father talking to him about the sunrises on the compound of the Denynso and how they were the most beautiful in all of the galaxy. Now that story carried even more meaning to him. His hand ran along the stone ledge that rose up around the former compound and suddenly he felt it dip. He looked at the wall and saw an opening he hadn't noticed before.

"What's this?" he asked Athan.

Athan came up to the wall and examined the opening, then shook his head.

"I don't know. I don't remember it from my time here."

"Nylek," Maxim called. "Do you know what this is?"

The Denynso approached the wall and stared at the gap in the stone. Maxim knew that like the other warriors of the clan Nylek had never been to the badlands. It had been forbidden just like the other areas outside of the compound and they had only seen it when Creia had brought them up to the top of the ledge and shown them the burning ground when they first returned from the human settlement. He hoped, though, that Nylek might have heard more about the badlands than he had. Perhaps his parents had told him stories that they had heard from their own parents, linking the generations to the years that the clan had been united and lived in the compound that was now the badlands.

Nylek shook his head, looking at Maxim with regret in his eyes.

"I'm sorry," he said. "I don't know. I don't know anything about the badlands. My family never talked about them."

"What is it, Maxim?" Ivy asked.

Maxim turned to his mate and held his arm open to her so that she could step up close to him. He gestured toward the opening in the stone.

"Do you have any idea what this might be?" he asked.

Ivy looked at the opening closely, her eyes narrowed as if trying to come up with something to tell him.

"It reminds me of some of the caverns on Earth," she said.

"Caverns?" Maxim asked.

Ivy nodded.

"They aren't all underground like Loralia's home. Some of them start at ground level or even up high on mountains and then they go deeper underground as you move further into them. There's one on the Denynso compound like that."

"There is?" Maxim asked.

Ivy nodded.

"That's how they first found the mirrored realm. Some of the warriors found a cave in the rock face of the ledge and when they went further into it they found a tunnel that led down into the caverns. They couldn't fit in the tunnel, though, and had to send the human women through it to find out what was in it."

"Were you there?" Maxim asked.

Ivy shook her head.

"No. It was before I came to the compound, before the warriors left on their exploration of the planet. Eden and the others told me about it."

"We need to go into it," Maxim said.

"We need to rest," Kyven protested. "We haven't slept in more than a day. We can't keep going without sleep."

Maxim looked at the others of the group and saw them nodding slightly. He looked down at Ivy who gazed into his eyes softly.

"I know that you are eager," she said, "but if we are going to stay safe and be able to do what needs to be done, whatever that is, then we have to have our strength. It is already morning. We need to get some rest and then we can keep going later."

Maxim nodded. He hadn't wanted to admit it to himself but he was feeling the pull of the hours of walking on his body and knew that getting some sleep would give him the strength and the energy that he needed to keep on their way. He didn't want to sacrifice the entire day, however, so he looked back at the rest of the group determinedly.

"We will set up camp and rest for a few hours. Just a few, though, and then we will keep going. We can't waste the daylight."

Maxim stepped through the opening in the rock and found himself in a cool, dark tunnel. He pulled out his bedroll and laid it down, then rested Ivy's beside it as the others stepped cautiously inside. Athan stretched a blanket across the tunnel to block as much of the sunlight from getting in as he could, and they all settled down to rest.

When Maxim's eyes opened he felt like he had been sleeping for years. His eyelids felt heavy and the rest of his body seemed to sink into the ground beneath him. Ivy curled against him, her head tucked against his chest and one of her legs draped over his. He leaned down to touch a kiss to the top of her head and she stirred slightly.

"We need to get going," he whispered.

Ivy nodded and they carefully disentangled themselves from one another. Around them Maxim saw the others starting to wake and gradually they got up and packed. Athan pulled the blanket down from where he had secured it, revealing the bright sunlight of midday. Maxim stood deep enough in the tunnel that the light barely touched him, but it illuminated the walls. That light allowed him so see carvings deep in the stone. He stepped toward them and touched them with his fingertips.

Athan saw what he was doing and came to his side.

"Do you know what these mean?" Maxim asked.

"I've seen them before," Athan told him, reaching up with his own hand to touch them. "Not here. They were in the inner quarters of some of the Order when I was younger. I can't decipher them fully, but I know that they are the same ones."

Maxim looked back down the tunnel, feeling drawn into the darkness.

"Could Creia have followed this tunnel?" he asked.

"He might have," Athan said.

"Nylek," Maxim said, "we need to get in touch with the queen. Can you please contact Mina?"

"Yes," Nylek responded.

Maxim felt slightly awkward watching as Nylek turned his eyes toward the wall and concentrated on the thoughts that he wanted his mate to hear. Even though it was something that the Denynso knew as commonplace, it still felt incredibly intimate to Maxim and he felt somewhat uncomfortable taking advantage of this connection, especially if it meant watching him as he did it.

Finally Nylek looked back to him again.

"I have her," he said. "What do you need me to ask her?"

"Please have her ask Theia to try to get in touch with Creia again," Maxim said. "We have found what appears to be a tunnel leading out of the badlands and I need her to ask him if he followed it."

Nylek nodded and went back to looking at the wall as he relayed the message to his mate back at the compound with Theia. They waited for several long moments with Maxim hoping that this would be the time when Theia would be able to get through to Creia. If they could confirm that he did follow this tunnel they might be able to get to him more quickly.

Nylek looked up at him, shaking his head.

"Theia isn't getting a response from the king," he said regretfully. "She said that she will keep trying, but that she hasn't been able to get to him again since he sent the message of 'badlands.'"

"Thank you, Nylek," Maxim said, "and thank Mina for me."

"What are we going to do?" Ivy asked.

"If Creia did go down this tunnel, it is going to be the only way that we are going to be able to find him and help him. If he didn't, though, and we follow it we could get lost and end up even further away from him. It could mean not being able to save him."

"We have to make a decision," Ivy said. "You have to choose."

Maxim looked at Athan. The older man looked into his eyes, the expression in his gaze telling Maxim that he didn't need this man's confirmation to know what he should do. He had to follow his heart and do what it told him.

3

———

Zyyr stared into the fire that Lila had built and cradled her closer to him. She curled familiarly into his arms, the curves of her body fitting into his as though each were crafted for the other. His body and mind felt satiated in a way that he could never have imagined, and now he truly understood what it was to be mated. It made sense to him now why the warriors were so aggressive about their mates while at the same time becoming more tender and softer with just the look of those women's eyes. Now that he had completed his bond with Lila he knew that he would never be able to be without her, and that he was irrevocably changed. She was all that mattered to him, and he would do anything to protect, comfort, and please her. Even as these thoughts rolled through his mind, however, something that she said lingered, bothering him.

"Lila?" he said.

"Hmmmm?" she said softly, the sound almost more of a sigh than it was an actual acknowledgement of him speaking to her.

"What did you mean when you said that your great-grandmother was different?"

Lila shifted slightly and Zyyr couldn't tell if it was because she wanted to get closer to him or if he had made her uncomfortable with the question.

"I'm sorry," he said, immediately regretting prying, especially in the calm and beautiful moment that they had been sharing. "I shouldn't have asked you that."

"No," Lila said as if trying to reassure him. "It's alright. I am the one who said that. You have every right to be curious. I'm just trying to decide what the best way to explain it would be. You see, I never really thought of her as strange. I guess that there are so many things about her that are like me that I didn't see her as odd the way that other people did. I just saw a woman who was beautiful and wonderful, a woman who always made me feel safe and understood. I was always comfortable when I was here with her. She never made me question the things about myself that other people did, or look at me with the curiosity in her eyes the way that I saw other people look at me. None of the things that were different about me when I was younger mattered to her."

"Maybe she loved you so much that she didn't notice that there was anything different about you," Zyyr offered, thankful that Lila wasn't angry with him and honored that she was sharing these things with him.

Lila laughed softly.

"No," she said, "she definitely noticed. In fact, I think that she might have noticed even more than other people did. Sometimes she would show me little things about her that weren't like anything I had ever seen in others and give me a little wink. She never said anything about it, but I somehow knew that I wasn't supposed to talk to other people about what she showed me or told me. It was like we had a special secret that was just about the two of us. Even though I knew that it was those secrets that made her an outcast and forced her to live out here away from the rest of the kingdom, they were the things that I loved the most about her."

"Why did they make her live out here? Just because she wasn't exactly like them?" Zyyr asked.

Lila sighed and shook her head.

"My mother told me that the people of the kingdom never told her that she had to live out here. They never forced her to. It was something that she chose to do because she knew how different she was and didn't want the other people to have any more opportunity to ridicule her than they already did."

The thought of the kind and welcoming Mikana people being cruel to one of their own simply because she was different in some ways didn't seem to fit in with his visions of these people, especially the soft and lovely Lila. He couldn't imagine people who were like her ousting another for no other reason that she didn't fit their exact concepts of what they should be.

"What did they ridicule her about?" Zyyr asked. "What was so different about her?"

"I never heard anyone be cruel about her," Lila admitted. "She never told me that anyone was mean or that that was why she lived out here. One time I asked her, and she told me that there were things that people didn't need to know because it might cause more harm than good, and she left it at that. When she said that to me I just thought that she was talking about me. After all, I was just a young child and she was already old. I thought that she was just worried that I wouldn't understand the things that she had gone through, even though I was so much like her, and that she worried if she told me that I would be afraid that the same types of things would happen to me."

"You don't think that anymore, do you?" Zyyr asked.

Lila shook her head and then turned in his arms so that she could look at him.

"What if she wasn't talking about me at all? What if she wasn't worried about what I would find out or what I knew, but about the other people in the kingdom?"

"What do you mean?"

"One time we were talking about my hair and she asked if my hair was like my mother's. My mother was the daughter of her son, my grandfather. She never went to see my great-grandmother. I never asked her why, but I know that it hurt my great-grandmother. When I told her that it wasn't, she just nodded, but there was something about the look on her face. It was almost like she was relieved. Like she didn't want to think that her granddaughter was differ-ent, too. Almost like she didn't want there to be someone who was different that was out among the rest of the people of the kingdom as often as she was. Maybe she didn't mean that there were things that I shouldn't know and that she wasn't going to tell me why she lived out here. Maybe that was the actual explanation. She was telling me why she lived here rather than in the kingdom itself. She lived here because the people of the kingdom didn't need to know some things about her."

Zyyr was starting to feel confused. He was trying to follow her, but he was struggling.

"Why was she asking about your hair?" he asked.

Though she was more beautiful than any other woman that he had ever seen, including the stunning Mikana women, there wasn't anything so distinctly different about her hair that he would have thought someone would question it. She looked at him strangely.

"You didn't notice?" she asked.

He shook his head and she tucked an arm under her thick mane of hair, lifting it up away from her back and turning it over. There among the other strands, glittering against them with their bold contrast, were strands of bright, shimmering silver.

Zyyr reached up to touch the strands of silver, his heart starting to pound in his chest as thoughts and questions raced through his mind. This was something that he hadn't seen on any of the others in the Mikana kingdom, but that he had seen before. He knew that shade of silver and the faint sparkle that came off of it. He didn't understand. How could Lila have these streaks of silver through her hair? What did they mean?

"Did your great-grandmother live in this house her whole life?" Zyyr asked.

Lila shook her head.

"No. Just as an adult."

"Where did she live when she was younger?"

"I don't know. No one was ever able to show me the house where she grew up. My grandfather only knows that he was born in this house. He never met his father."

Zyyr knew that what he had just learned was important, but he didn't know why. There was something about the information that struck him and lingered in his mind, creating an urgency to find Maxim and tell him everything that Lila had said.

"Lila," he said, turning her around so that he could take her hands and stare into her eyes, wanting to ensure that she was listening to him and understanding what he was saying to her. "Do you trust me?"

"Of course, I do," she answered, her eyes narrowing slightly as she looked at him.

"I need to find Maxim and tell him what you have told me."

She shook her head slightly.

"Why?" she asked. "I told you those things in confidence."

"I know that, Darling. I know you did, and I wouldn't tell anyone if I didn't think that it was important. There are things that Maxim, the Denynso, and even the humans are trying to understand, and I think that what you told me about your great-grandmother might be another piece for them."

"What do you think it means?" she asked.

"I'm not completely sure," he admitted. "I just know that it seems important and if there is even the slightest chance that that information could help them, we want them to have it. It could mean more to this planet than either of us know."

Lila looked as though she were contemplating what he had just said to her and then nodded.

"But why Maxim? I thought that a warrior named Pyra was the leader of the Denynso."

"Just the warriors," Zyyr told her, "and I have withdrawn my loyalty to him and given it to Maxim. I believe in him and want to do whatever I can to help him."

She nodded again.

"I trust you," she said. "If you think that what I've told you could help in some way, then you can tell Maxim."

Zyyr leaned forward and kissed her.

"Thank you," he said.

He climbed to his feet and dressed as quickly as he could. When he was finished he rushed out of the house to run back toward the houses so that he could find Maxim,

Lila right beside him. They searched the houses and the common areas, asking everyone who they passed if they had seen Maxim, his human partner, or his brother. No one seemed to know where they were or where they had gone, and Zyyr started to feel a sense of panic rising in him.

Finally they found Oro, the other Denynso who had traveled with them from the settlement to the Mikana kingdom. He stood with some of the Mikana men in one of the clearings, eating fruit out of a basket much like the one that Lila had brought with her.

"Oro," Zyyr called to him, gesturing for him to come away from the others and talk with him in private.

"Do you know where Maxim is?" Zyyr asked.

"No," Oro said. "Is everything alright?"

"We need to find him," Zyyr said. "I have something that I need to tell him."

"I know where his mother lives," Oro offered.

"Let's go."

Zyyr followed Oro through the kingdom, confident that they would arrive at Maxim's mother's house and find him there with her and Ivy. When a woman opened the door, however, the strained look on her face told him that she was not going to be able to help him. He had to do whatever he could to try to find out, though.

"Hello," he said. "My name is Zyyr. I traveled from the human settlement here with Maxim and Ivy."

"Yes," the woman who Zyyr assumed was Maxim and Kyven's mother said.

"Do you know where they are?" he asked.

She shook her head, looking weakened by his words.

"I don't know," she said, emotion in her voice making the words sound somewhat distant. "They left."

"Left?" Zyyr demanded. "When?"

"Yesterday," the woman said. I don't know where they went."

"Was it just Maxim and Ivy?" Zyyr asked.

"No," she said. "Kyven, Emerie, and Athan were with him, too."

Zyyr turned to Oro with the feeling of panic rising in his chest again. The warriors met eyes and Zyyr knew that without words even passing between them their decision was made. They had to find Maxim. If he left the kingdom it was for a very specific, very serious reason, and they needed to be with him.

4

Pain radiated through Creia's eyes as he struggled to open them. The sharp, piercing pain came as a relief. He had been unconscious for quite some time and briefly thought that the life had finally drained out of him. The pain came as a sudden, intense, and welcome reminder that he was still alive. No matter how long he had been latched to the table, staring into the screen that was in front of him, Ryan had not yet succeeded in killing him. He could continue to fight.

The hooded creature had not been back since the last time that he put the screen over Creia's eyes. This had forced him to watch Ryan as he moved through his lab, performing strange experiments and occasionally going over to the thing in the tank in the corner, glaring in at it as if examining it for some reason that may apply to whatever he was trying to accomplish with the tubes, vials, and bottles strewn across the tables. Sometimes he would open a notebook and scribble feverishly in it, his garbled mutterings to himself loud enough that Creia could hear his voice, but indecipherable as actually understandable words. That is what he was doing now, hunched over the notebook and writing so quickly that Creia could see the ink from the fresh words spreading across his hand as it slid across the page.

The process fascinated Creia. Though the Denynso were known for rejecting the technologies that many other species had and relied largely instead on craftsmanship, he knew that the humans didn't follow the same way of life. Instead they seemed to thrive on advancement and pushed to progress their technology and way of life as fast as possible. Some of the things that the human women had described to him were almost unfathomable, but it was the very reality that those items existed that made watching Ryan use a nearly primitive form of recording his thoughts oddly intriguing.

Suddenly Ryan stopped and dropped the pen he was holding. It hit the table and rolled across the smooth metal surface, tipping over the edge and falling to the floor. Something about the gesture sent a thrill of fear through Creia. He knew deep within him that the people he treasured the most were in serious danger, but there was nothing he could do to help them. He was tied to the table so that he couldn't move and his body was weakening more and more with each passing hour. He had already gone without food or water for long enough that he could feel everything within him failing. He wanted desperately to reach out to Theia, but with the diodes connected to his head and the screen in front of his eyes, he couldn't be sure that the thoughts he would send her would be completely his own. He knew that she had tried to speak to him. Even though he had forced his mind to block her out to protect her, he could feel the pull within his heart that told him that she had been thinking of him, reaching out to him with her mind. He wondered what she had wanted to say to him, but couldn't let his mind wander or it would take away the last grasps of control he had.

Ryan looked up at the camera sharply and Creia saw the wildness in his eyes. The man seemed to be slipping further and further into insanity, losing his own control over his mind and allowing his intense thoughts to take over him completely.

"DNA," Ryan said, taking a few fast steps toward the camera so that he was right up against it and Creia could only see his eyes. "Do you know what that is?"

Creia didn't know if he should respond. It didn't seem as though Ryan were truly taking to him, but part of him feared what may happen if the scientist intended for him to respond but he didn't. Ryan took a step back so that Creia could see the entirety of his face again and tilted his head.

"Hmmm?" he said questioningly. "Do you Denynso know anything more than war and bedding women indiscriminately?"

Creia squirmed at the accusation. He knew the reputation that his men had throughout the galaxy, and much of it was well earned, but the way that Ryan said it made him feel angry and provoked.

"I know of DNA," Creia managed to force past the pain in his dry, tight throat.

"Good," Ryan said with a mirthless chuckle. "Then you understand why I had to send Eden to your planet."

Confusion washed over Creia.

"You already told me that you sent her to get the blood of the Denynso. You sent her for Pyra's blood and with the hope that we would capture her and kill her."

"Yes, yes," Ryan said, waving his hand as if brushing away something inconsequential. "I did hope that if she wasn't able to get the blood of your most fearsome warrior that you would take her and punish her the way that everyone knows the Denynso love to punish. Not only would it be giving her something that she deserved, but it would mobilize Earth's government and force them to see you and your kind as nothing but a galactic threat." He gave another laugh. "And, of course, we all know how that would have turned out for you. Earth does have its way of going after those who they think have wronged them."

Creia found it strange the way that Ryan was speaking of Earth and its inhabitants in such a disconnected, cold way, but his mind was already struggling through the impairment of the exhaustion, starvation, and dehydration to understand anything that the man was saying to him so he couldn't stop to try to dwell on his motivations.

"You know," Ryan said, bringing a finger to his lips briefly as if the cruel smile there indicated he was pondering new thoughts running through his mind, "that is how this all began. Come to think of it, it was because of that little tendency of Earth's government that any of this happened at all. I suppose my mind just went right back to the beginning."

"What do you mean?" Creia asked, his voice soft and almost inaudible over the sound of Ryan's laughter. "How what all began?"

"DNA," Ryan said again, the laughter suddenly gone from his voice as he stared directly into the camera in a way that told Creia with certainty that just as he could see the scientist in his lab, Ryan could see him wherever he was secured to the table. "It's like little blocks. You know? Like the toys that little ones play with." He walked back a few steps so that he was standing at a table and grabbed a handful of small glass cubes from a box. He started to stack them into several individual towers. "You can make them into anything. You just start building and suddenly you have created something." He paused and looked at the towers of blocks contemplatively. "Why do those blocks always have to be the same, though? What would happen if you took them," he picked the top block off of one of the towers with his thumb and forefinger and dropped it into the top of one of the other towers, "and found out what else you could build with them?"

A horrifying reality started to form in Creia's mind and he felt the desperation to escape building through him again.

"What have you done, Ryan?" he demanded. Ryan continued to play with the tiny glass cubes, giggling to himself as he redistributed the cubes among the towers and then took them and started creating new towers. "What have you done?"

Ryan looked up.

"It wasn't me," he said, the look on his face suddenly innocent in a way that bordered on disturbing. "I didn't start this. I only intend to complete it. I've had to be so patient. So incredibly patient. It is all going to pay off soon, though." He smiled and Creia felt a sick feeling twist through his stomach. "Things are working out even better than I had originally planned and I am being rewarded handsomely for the sacrifices I have made and the devotion that I had shown all these years. You see, things don't always work out the way that you intend them to. Sometimes what you think you're building," he turned his attention back to one of the towers and used the back of his hand to push it over so that the cubes scattered across the surface of the table and down onto the floor, "topples. Or perhaps you come up with a better idea but all of your blocks are already being used.

Whatever the reason, it can be incredibly frustrating. There've been times when I felt like all of this was for nothing and that I would never be able to accomplish what I had planned to do. Then I just kept working. I sent Eden to Uoria to secure the DNA and the potent elements within the blood of your Pyra. She didn't accomplish that, or so I thought. Now I have access to something far more powerful than I could have ever imagined." He picked up one of the cubes and stared into it. "I have a hybrid baby and the milk that nourishes it."

5

———

"**I**s everything alright?" Lila asked.

Zyyr gave her an intense look and she noticed for the first time that his once green eyes were now a vibrant shade of orange. She could see in that stare that everything was most certainly not alright and that Zyyr was deeply troubled by what Oro had said to him.

"We have to leave," Zyyr told her.

Panic with a sharp edge of pain coursed through her and Lila resisted the urge to take a step back.

"Why?" she asked.

"Maxim is no longer in the kingdom," Zyyr explained. "He left with his mate, his brother, and two others. We have to find them."

"What is it about what I told you that upsets you so much?" Lila asked.

She couldn't understand what she had said about her great-grandmother that had gotten to Zyyr so much that he shifted from a passionate and tender man to one who seemed distracted and obsessive. The anxiety he was feeling radiated off of him and it made Lila feel as though she could barely breathe. Zyyr reached out and took both of her hands in his, pulling them up so that he could clutch them against his heart.

"I wish that I knew of a way to tell you," he said. "I wish that I could make you understand, but even I don't understand completely what's happening or what has happened. I can only tell you that we have seen so much more in the time that we have been out of the compound than we ever could have imagined, and every day it seems that we are finding out more. While I wish that it was all good, the truth is that it's not. We're worried that some of the things that we've found out could mean that there is serious danger for everyone on this planet. If we can find out what that is, we might be able to stop whatever it is from getting worse, or from happening at all."

"And you think that my great-grandmother has something to do with it?" she asked.

"I don't know," Zyyr said, shaking his head, "but it is something that I feel that we need to talk to Maxim about. Most of the Denynso warriors are not on the planet right now, but Maxim is and so is our king, Creia. They might have more insight into what you told me and be able to find the connections to everything else that we have uncovered better than I can."

Lila was trying to understand what Zyyr was saying, but it all seemed so strange to her. She knew that her great-grandmother had been different and had spent her life isolated from the others of the kingdom, but she couldn't fathom what impact that could have on anything that the Denynso or Maxim had learned. Idella had been reclusive nearly her whole life as far as Lila knew. Like most of the Mikana women she had lived in the kingdom her entire life and had not left it. She had had one son and then lived to a fairly remarkable age alone in the small home that she adored.

She tried to remember everything that she had told Zyyr when they were alone together in her great-grandmother's house, trying to find something, anything in her words that would have triggered the response that he had had. Suddenly she remembered telling him what her great-grandmother had said about living out in the house away from the rest of the kingdom, first with her son, and then alone after her son grew older and began his own life. Idella had told Lila that there were things that people didn't need to know because they might cause more harm than good. She was certain now that she hadn't been chastising Lila's question. Instead, she had been answering her. Her great-grandmother had stayed out in that house away from the others so that the people of the kingdom wouldn't find out something about her.

She rested a hand on Zyyr's arm and lifted her eyes to his.

"I need to show you something."

"I'm sorry, Lila, but I have to find Maxim."

"This is important, Zyyr," she told him. "I think that it might help you."

She saw him nod and they started toward Idella's house again, Oro following close behind them. When they arrived she closed the door tightly and pulled the drapes. Though she hadn't seen anyone come around the house in many years, she didn't want to take any chances that this would be the time that someone would wander out through the orchards for a peek into the windows of the strange and storied home.

Once confident that the house was secure, she walked over to the fireplace and counted out the bricks in the pattern that Idella had taught her when she was just a child. It was a game to her then, but now that she was older Lila realized just how serious it was that her great-grandmother had to be so secretive. She identified the right brick and wriggled it out of place. Inside was a gemstone, dulled by years and embedded so deeply into the stone around it that Lila could barely see it. She felt it with the pads of her fingers and the pressed it, holding it for a few moments just as she had been instructed. When she realized it she heard the dull scratching sound of the fireplace moving out of place and easing forward a few inches. Lila stepped carefully up to the edge, relieved that she and Zyyr had extinguished the flames before they left in search of Oro, and tucked her fingers behind it.

"Can you help me?" she asked over her shoulder.

There had been a time when even her small great-grandmother had been able to move the fireplace aside with ease, but that had been many years before and the time had settled the stones into place so much that they resisted being moved again. It was almost as if the house itself was trying to protect the secrets that the small room behind the fireplace concealed. The two warriors came up to the fireplace and tucked their hands around the edge just as she had. In one motion the stone moved out of place, revealing the door behind it.

Hoping that it would move more easily than the fireplace had, Lila grasped the large metal ring that acted as a handle and tugged it. The door relented fairly quickly and she pulled it open. The smell of forgotten years and captured breaths came out of the space toward them and Lila waited a tense, nervous moment before walking inside. Behind her Zyyr illuminated a light stick and held it up above her head so that the glow splashed across the floor in front of her and helped her to see as she moved further inside. Soon she found the lamp that had always sat on the small table inside the room and lit the flame inside, adjusting it so that it would burn brightly enough for them to see in the space, but not so much that it would do away with the precious oil within it, the last oil that Idella had ever put inside.

"What is this place?" Zyyr asked.

"My great-grandmother used to bring me in here when I was younger. It always felt like a secret passage, like this was where she could store all of the treasures of the world and no one would find them. Now, though, I wonder if it was her that she wanted to make sure that no one found."

"Why do you say that?" Oro asked.

"I was thinking about what I told Zyyr about my great-grandmother. Idella was an amazing woman. Perhaps the single most incredible person I have ever known. Yet she always stayed right here, and if anyone came close to the house, I would see her getting closer to the fireplace. Now that you've told me that there are secrets and dangers on Uoria that we don't understand, I wonder if she was preparing to hide in this room. Maybe she knew of one of the dangers and wanted to be able to come in here whenever she felt threatened."

"So that others wouldn't find out and cause more harm than they could good," Zyyr said.

Lila nodded.

"Is this what you wanted to show us?" Oro asked.

Lila stepped further into the room, holding up the lamp so that she could look at the shelves built along one wall in the small space.

"Yes, but the room isn't all. There's something else that I need to show you."

She saw the box sitting in the center of the middle shelf just as it always had been and reached out to carefully take it down. She carried it over to the small table and rested it reverently on the surface.

"I never got to know my great-grandfather," she said, pausing with her hands on the top of the box, "and there wasn't much that Idella would tell me about him. She would only say that he was the greatest love that she would ever have and that he was the reason that she was able to have the life that she did. She said that he was the only reason that she was able to have a family the way that she did."

"Of course he is if he was her son's father," Oro said.

Lila shook her head.

"I think it's more than that," she said. "The way that she always said it didn't seem like she meant it because their son was the only child that they had and that she wouldn't have had him had she not found my great-grandfather. Instead it seemed more like she was saying that without him she never would have had a family at all. Like he ensured that she was able to have a life." She took a breath. "This box was my great-grandmother's most prized possession. She used to take it down when we were in here and look at what was inside. She told me once that her husband carved it for her and that she used to keep their love letters in it."

"Is that what's in it now?" Zyyr asked.

She shook her head, feeling tears pricking the corners of her eyes as she thought of those letters. She could still remember the way that the paper felt beneath her fingertips and the curves of the words across the page.

"No," she said. "When she died I didn't think that she should be without them. They were with her when we buried her. I knew that I was perhaps the only other person who knew about those letters, so I made sure that they were tucked out of sight so that she could carry them privately with her and no one would ever know what she said to him or what he said to her."

"Did you ever read the letters?" Zyyr asked.

Lila shook her head again.

"No," she answered. "Idella would read them and then she would place them aside and go back into the box for this."

She reached into the box and withdrew the blue leather bound book she had seen at some of her favorite moments throughout her life. These were the moments when she was able to spend quiet time with her great-grandmother, the one person who made her feel like she belonged.

"What is that?" Zyyr asked.

Lila sat and lowered the book to her lap, running her hand along the cover. It had been so long since she had seen that book, but if she searched the corners of her mind she could still hear Idella's voice reading the story inside to her. She opened the cover and ran her fingertips along the words on the title. It simply said *Fairy Tale.*

"This is a book that my great-grandmother read to me. She said that it was her very favorite fairy tale."

"What is it about?" Zyyr asked.

There was a slight edge to his voice that told Lila that he was feeling impatient, wondering what it was that had led her to bring him and Oro to this hidden room. She turned the title page and looked at the detailed illustration on the first page of the book. It was a beautiful and lush scene of a place that Lila had never seen except for on those pages.

"This book," she said, turning the page again and looking at the next illustration, "tells the story of a woman who was born in a strange and foreign land and cruelly mistreated by an evil master. She often wondered who she really was and where she had come from, but the man who kept her would tell her that it didn't matter if she ever knew because the only reason that she was alive was to continue the work on a large and complex project." She turned the page again and looked at the stark image of a cold-looking room that had walls lined with tanks. "This woman thought that she was going to live out her life trapped there, kept for this evil man's whims. She was becoming an adult, coming to an age that she had always feared because it was the age at which the women that lived alongside her would be taken from that space and she would never see them again. She didn't know what was happening to them or even who took them, but she was terrified that it was going to happen to her."

"What happened?" Zyyr asked.

"It was nearly time for her to come of age and she was moved out of the space that she knew into a room connected to it. That is when she met a wonderful young man. He cared for her and prepared her for the experience that lay ahead of her, but wouldn't tell her what it was. She knew when she looked into his eyes that he was afraid of what he knew and didn't want to tell her anything about it. One night, just two days before she was to come of age, the young man came to her room and took her. He helped her escape from the building where she had been born and that she knew her entire life. They ran away together and he told her the story of how she came to be." She turned the page again and showed him a picture of two people sitting beneath a tall, overhanging tree that was nothing like Lila had ever seen. "He told her that she was not like other women and that this planet that she had known all of her life was not the one that she was intended to live on. It was not the home of her ancestors."

"Where was she?" Oro asked.

Lila could hear that the fascination was starting to build in the men and she continued on, letting the magic interwoven in the words of the story to draw them in so that they could understand what she needed them to know.

"It doesn't say," Lila said, "but the illustrations are not like anything that I have ever seen in the kingdom or in the drawings done by those who have left the kingdom and explored other parts of Uoria." She turned the page again and showed them a picture of the two stepping onto a small ship. "The young man told her that he wanted to bring her back to the planet where she should have been born, and yet would never have been born at all. She was afraid, but she had fallen so deeply in love with him that she knew that she could never resist him. They got onto a strange craft and it took them into the stars. It was something that this young woman couldn't have imagined. She had lived her entire life thinking that there was nothing beyond the building and now she was traveling off of the planet with the promise of a new life."

"I don't understand," Zyyr said. "What does it mean that he was going to bring her to the planet where she should have been born, but where she never would have been born at all?"

Lila smiled. It was the same question that she had asked her great-grandmother when she was young and would hear the story. Idella would smile at her and continue the story, and it was not until she got older that she began to understand it. She did the same now, turning the page again and letting her eyes move adoringly over her favorite picture of the book. It was of the young woman stepping into an incredibly lush and beautiful glade, welcomed by lovely people with flowing hair the same shimmering silver as half of the woman's.

"When they arrived on the new planet the man brought her to a place filled with people who looked very much like her. They welcomed her and began to teach her their ways. She felt comfortable there, but it still seemed as though part of her were missing. It was a strange feeling, something that she had never experienced before, but it was as though she was suddenly aware of a longing, a deep draw that wanted to lure her to something that she didn't even know she was missing. After a short time with the silver-haired people, the man told the young woman that she had somewhere else to go now. They left the beautiful place and traveled across the planet for some time. Finally they arrived at a kingdom that seemed so different from the place where they had just been, but also felt strangely calming and familiar to the young woman. This was the home of the young man's kind. This kingdom was less lush and natural than the first place, but rather filled with technology and people so incredibly lovely that it was almost breathtaking to look at them. Here she felt like the piece of her that she hadn't known was missing was suddenly restored.

Here she settled with the man. Though most of the people of the kingdom were kind and welcoming to her, there were some, a very few, who seemed to know that she was different. This made her worry that she was something that could put the others at risk. She wasn't like them in many ways and found herself wanting to hide these differences. She withdrew from the rest of the people and created a home deep in the woods where she began her family. She never spoke of what made her different and there she remained throughout the rest of her life, knowing that she was home but still carrying in her heart the spirit of the silver-haired people that she had left behind."

Lila closed the book and ran her hand lovingly across

the cover again. She felt tears forming in the back of her throat as she thought of her great-grandmother. The sound of Idella's voice faded from her mind and Lila longed to feel the soft kiss that she would always press to her great-granddaughter's forehead after reading the story to her. It was as though that kiss was an affirmation, an encouragement for her to take more out of the fantastical tale than just the delight of hearing it. Though she had never told her great-grandmother, Lila had always put great meaning into that story and knew that there was far more in the words than Idella had ever admitted.

"Is that book about your great-grandmother?" Zyyr asked.

Lila nodded.

"I think so. She never told me that, but I don't see how it couldn't be. She used to touch my hair as she read it to me, like she was trying to point out the silver streaks in my hair that were just like the ones in hers. Hers had far more silver in it than mine, at least when I was young, and she never fully looked like the other people of the kingdom. I can't tell you exactly what it was, but there was just something about her that was slightly different. Of course, to me she was just my great-grandmother. As I got older and heard this story over and over, and then after she died and I read it to myself to feel close to her, I really started to understand what she was trying to tell me with it."

"She didn't want to tell you where she came from or what had happened to her because she was afraid that the others in the kingdom might find out and it would put them all at risk," Oro said.

"I think so," Lila repeated, nodding. "I think that she used this fairy tale as a way to ensure that I would know the true history of my family. I'm the last of my bloodline, and if I didn't know what had truly happened, it would all be lost. I believe that she hoped I would understand and ensure that I carried it on to any future generations. Even if it was just through the fairy tale."

"No," Zyyr said. "No. It can't be just the fairy tale. The reason that she told you that story so many times was so that you could know who your family really is. Your great-grandmother recognized in you the features and characteristics that made her different. She knew that one day you would realize that they were more than you even know and she wanted you to be ready for it."

"What do you mean?"

Lila saw Zyyr give Oro a meaningful glance and then look back at her.

"You said that there were times when your great-grandmother would do things that were different and that she would smile at you, like you two had a special secret."

"Yes," Lila said.

"What would she do? What were some of those special things that she seemed to be able to do but that others couldn't?"

Lila thought back. These were the types of private moments that she had shared with her great-grandmother and never told anyone else about. They had been such an element of her time with Idella that it was difficult to separate them from other parts of their time together and exactly explain what it was that Idella did that was so different. She gave a sigh.

"I don't really know how to explain it. It was like she could make people believe things were happening that weren't. That's really the only way that I can describe it. She always knew exactly what someone was feeling and if they needed something, and sometimes she would do things that would make it as though she could make them see things or have things disappear."

Zyyr looked at Oro again and Oro nodded.

"Lila, when those things happened, was your great-grandmother holding anything?"

"What do you mean?"

Zyyr reached out and touched the book in Lila's lap.

"May I?" he asked.

Lila nodded and released the book so that he could pick it up. She watched as he carefully opened the cover and turned the pages until he came to a specific picture, then turned the book so that she could look at it. He rested his finger on the illustration.

"This picture is what I'm guessing is the place where the silver-haired people lived and they are greeting the young woman. They are handing her something. If we are right and this young woman is actually your great-grandmother, this might be a picture of them giving her a gift that she carried with her and used for the rest of her life. Do you recognize it?"

Lila had never made the connection before, but Zyyr pointing out that image made her remember something from her childhood with Idella. She stood and rushed out of the small room behind the fireplace, heading directly to the bedroom where Idella had slept and taken her last breath. She opened the small drawer in the table beside her bed and moved aside a small stack of handkerchiefs. Beneath them, just where she had tucked it years before after Idella's death when she had taken over the home, was a tiny silver compact. She withdrew it carefully and turned to the men who had followed her.

"This," she said, holding the compact up for them to see. "She used to wear this around her neck. When those strange things happened, she was always holding it. I never really thought of it before."

She heard Zyyr draw in a breath and his face take on an expression that she couldn't quite decipher.

"Do you believe that what this book says is actually about your great-grandmother?" he asked.

"Yes," Lila said, more confident about it now than she ever had been.

"Then we need to go."

"What? I don't understand."

Zyyr had run back toward the room behind the fireplace and Lila followed him, watching as he picked up the book and carried it out of the room and toward the table in the center of the house. He rested the book onto the table and flipped through the pages again.

"The young woman, your great-grandmother, and the man, her husband ---"

"Idella and Finean."

Lila felt a rush of strength and peace come over her as she said the names of her great-grandparents, finally acknowledging that this story was her history, the legacy that they had left for her. She felt connected to them in a new and powerful way, as though she were giving them a voice again after they had to go so long without one.

"Idella and Finean traveled back and forth from the place of the silver-haired people to the Mikana kingdom more than once. The first time that they came to the kingdom they walked and it took days of travel. The second time they visited they used some of the technology that the Mikana used at the time to travel and it was much shorter. But the last time that they made the journey, right before Idella decided that she could never go back there, they didn't use the vehicles. They traveled through tunnels that got them there almost as fast as the vehicles would have. Where are the tunnels?"

"I have no idea. I never knew of any tunnels."

"If the rest of this story is true, then those tunnels have to exist. At least they did when Idella was younger. Maybe that's where Maxim went."

"What do you mean?" Oro asked.

"Maxim is on a mission to understand what happened to his father. I don't know everything that he knows, but I have heard him talking to his mate, Ivy, about some of the things that he has uncovered."

"He talked about it a lot on the way here from the compound," Oro agreed. "He wouldn't explain it all and we haven't seen him since we got here."

"So you think that the secrets that he is keeping have to do with my great-grandmother?" Lila asked.

The thought was overwhelming in a way. Her entire life she had only thought of her great-grandmother as being different, but still her great-grandmother. There was nothing more extensive to it than that. Now she was realizing that the story of Idella and why she was so different than the others had much further-reaching implications that she could have ever imagined.

"They might. That is all we have to go on right now. He could have found out the same things that we just did and gone to this place, where the silver-haired people lived."

"Lived?" Lila asked, emphasizing the fact that Zyyr had used the past tense to refer to them.

His eyes grew troubled and a darkness came over his face that made her nervous. He gestured to the compact in her hand.

"We have seen a compact like that before," he told her. "Two of them. One was given to another warrior named

Bannack by his mate Loralia. It belonged to her father. The other is hers. If they are the same..."

His voice trailed off and Zyyr drew in a breath. Lila didn't ask him to continue. She didn't want to hear the rest. Her hand wrapped tightly around the compact and she held it close to her.

"How do we find the tunnels?"

6

———

Creia thrashed against his binds, fighting them with the wave of fury that gave him new strength. He knew that Ryan was referring to Pyra, Eden, and Lysander, and the thought filled him with an anger more intense than he had ever experienced.

"That is my son," he growled, "and his mate, and my grandson. He is not a hybrid."

The word came out of his mouth like poison, sounding vile and making his muscles tense. Ryan laughed.

"Of course he is," he said. "He is Denynso and he is human. He is not either one and he is both."

"Eden is Denynso now," Creia said.

He didn't know why, but it seemed that perhaps if he convinced Ryan that Eden was not truly human any longer, Ryan's aggression toward her, and perhaps his desire what-ever it is that he planned on doing with her, Pyra, and their son, would fade.

"She was born human," Ryan said. "She was human when she conceived the child. That means that the baby has human DNA. I couldn't care less what species she is. I don't need her for anything but the milk that she produces. The rest of her is useless to me now."

The words sent panic through him and Creia fell silent. He knew now that his arguments were going to do nothing for him. He didn't know what Ryan had intended for the family, but he did know that it was not the first time that he had done it, and that he wouldn't be influenced by anything that the Denynso king had to say. Creia's eyes closed and he forced himself to reach deeply into his mind and release the blocks that he had put up. He focused in on Theia, gathering all of his strength and determination to reach out to her, to plead for her help.

"Theia," he thought. "Theia, please, are you there?"

Creia heard Ryan give a short laugh.

"Are you finally dead?" he asked. "Have you given up?"

Creia ignored the taunt and continued to focus on Theia, pushing past the defenses he had put up to try to reach his mate. The silence that greeted him was almost painful as it settled in his chest and seemed to swell with each second that passed.

"Theia," he thought again. "Theia, please, talk to me."

"Theia."

The cup that was in Theia's hand fell from her fingertips and crashed the floor, the water inside splashing out and spreading across the smooth stone. She gasped, her hand coming to her mouth.

"What is it?" Mina asked, rushing to her and kneeling down in front of the queen's chair to look into her face.

Theia didn't respond. Instead she closed her eyes so that she could focus harder on the soft, almost inaudible words she thought she had heard.

"Theia, please."

The words came again and she was positive then that they were in Creia's voice. Hearing her mate again after days of not being able to get in touch with him made her sob with relief.

"Creia, I'm here," she thought. "I'm here."

There was a moment of silence and she felt panic building within her.

"Theia."

She gave another sob at the sound of his response and reached out for Mina's hand. The girl took it and squeezed it comfortingly even though the queen knew that she didn't know yet what was happening.

"Oh, my love, I've been so worried about you," Theia thought. "Where are you?"

"I need you to listen to me," Creia said.

The sternness in his voice brought the smile from Theia's lips.

"What is it?" she replied. "What's wrong?"

"Is Maxim in the compound with you?" he asked.

"No," Theia told him. "He left searching for you. I can communicate with him, though. He brought Nylek with him and I have Mina with me."

"That was brilliant. I need you to tell him that I have been captured. I am being held somewhere outside of the badlands, but I'm not sure where."

"Are you alright?" Theia asked, terrified now that she knew that her mate was not just away, but in danger.

"I am alive," Creia responded. "That's the most I can say for now. Pyra, Eden, and Lysander are in serious danger."

"But they are on Earth," Theia argued.

"I know. Ryan ordered my capture. I don't know who actually did it or where I am, but it was done for Ryan. He told me himself that he has been waiting for Pyra's blood and now that he has the three of them he will be able to work on a project that he has been waiting to do since before Eden even came to Uoria."

"What project?"

"I'm not sure, but I know that they are in danger. Is Maxim alone?"

"No. He has Ivy, his brother, a human woman, and Athan with him."

"Athan," Creia muttered.

She knew that the name carried meaning for Creia.

"How will they find you?" she asked.

"Get in contact with them. When you are in touch, I will give them all of the information that I can. "

MAXIM WATCHED Athan as he walked ahead of them, running his fingers along the walls of the tunnel and using the illumination from the light stick that Maxim held to decipher the symbols carved into the stone. The frequency of the carvings had changed very suddenly and Maxim had the strange sense that they had traveled a very far distance in only a few moments.

"Do you understand what they mean?" Maxim asked.

Athan shook his head.

"Not all of them," he said. "Some of them, like these," he ran his hand along one section of the wall, "are familiar. This one says 'war'. This one says 'ally'. A few of these are names or family symbols. This one you might recognize, Maxim."

Maxim stepped forward and looked at the symbol that Athan was pointing to, tucked among many other symbols carved into the stone.

"My father," he said softly.

Athan nodded.

"Is your symbol here?" Maxim asked.

"No," Athan said. "I was never in this tunnel."

"I thought that you were always with my father when you went into battle."

"I was," Athan said, sounding slightly confused. "We stayed together when we fought so that we could back each other up or be able to tell our families what happened if..."

His voice trailed off as Maxim felt his spine stiffen.

"Could someone else have carved it?" he asked.

"I don't think so," Athan said. "Each symbol is very specific and the way that each member of the Order writes it is unique. Your father wrote this symbol."

Maxim looked at the name symbols more closely and noticed that they had been carved calmly, as though written there when the men were relaxing rather than in a hurried, hectic way. It seemed as though they were written out of the desire to entertain themselves rather than out of fear or the desire to be noticed.

"If you were always with him, how did he write his symbol here?"

Athan shook his head, continued to outline the carving with his fingertips.

"Maxim!"

The shout of his name from behind him caused Maxim to turn sharply. Nylek was rushing toward him down the tunnel. He, Kyven, and Emerie had been moving more slowly down the tunnel and Maxim hadn't realized how far behind them they had gotten.

"What is it, Nylek?" Maxim asked.

"Where did you go?" the warrior asked, panting as he stopped in front of him.

Maxim felt Ivy's hand wrap around his arm tightly.

"What do you mean?" Maxim asked. "We've been right ahead of you."

"Did you find him?" Kyven shouted moments before appearing in the glow of Maxim's light stick.

"He is right here," Nylek said.

"Kyven, we were only a few steps ahead of you. What's wrong?"

Kyven was shaking his head, a frightened look in his eyes.

"You were there and then you weren't. We had paused for a few seconds to drink some water and when we looked up again we couldn't see your light or hear you. It was like you disappeared."

"The tunnel," Ivy muttered.

"What?" Maxim asked.

She looked up at him, her hand tightening further.

"Remember when I was telling you about what the women told me about the tunnel that led down into the mirrored realm where they met Loralia?"

Maxim nodded.

"Yes. You said that it was like this one."

"Exactly. They said that there was a portal in that tunnel that led them down into the realm much faster than they would have been able to go without it. In just a matter of seconds they were able to get a distance that would likely have taken them an hour or more to walk."

As if the words have galvanized him, Athan took off running down the tunnel. Maxim followed, holding Ivy's hand with a sudden sense of concern that if he didn't keep her close he could lose her in the tunnel. After a few moments he could see sunlight ahead of him and they burst out of the tunnel into a quiet, empty space that looked like the forgotten remnants of an old compound.

"What is this place?" Kyven asked as he followed Maxim out of the tunnel and into the sunlight.

Maxim shook his head.

"Athan, do you know where we are?"

"I don't," Athan said, taking a few steps forward and looking around. "I've never been here before. It looks so familiar."

"It looks like the Denynso compound," Ivy said.

Maxim heard Nylek gasp behind him and turned to see the Denynso reaching out for him as if trying to get his attention.

"Nylek?" he said. "What is it?"

"Mina," the warrior said. "She says that Theia needs to talk to you."

Maxim saw Ivy's eyes widen and the other members of the travel group stepped in closer together.

"Alright," Maxim said.

Nylek nodded and turned his eyes away from them.

"She says that she heard from Creia."

Maxim felt a spike in his heartrate.

"Where is he?" Maxim asked

Nylek shook his head.

"She doesn't know. He says that he was captured."

"By who?" Maxim demanded.

"He doesn't know," Nylek said. "Theia wants to know where we are."

"Tell her that we don't know. Describe this place to her."

A few moments later Nylek nodded.

"Creia says that we are in the old Denynso compound. This is where he was when he was captured."

Ivy's hand squeezed Maxim's and he squeezed back.

"Ask him where he was when he was captured."

Maxim felt his heart pounding in his chest as he waited for the response from Creia. The moments dragged past, piling onto one another, intensifying his anxiety.

"Theia says that the king is weak. She is having difficulty understanding him. He said that he was exploring one of the houses and that he was taken by a hooded creature. He doesn't know where he is or how far he was taken from the compound. He only knows that Pyra, Eden, and Lysander are in serious danger, and he thinks that the others may be as well. He needs us to find him as quickly as possible. He says even if he doesn't survive, he needs us to do everything we can to help them."

"Tell her that we will find him," Maxim said.

"There's one more message from Creia," Nylek said, and then paused as if waiting for the message from Mina. "There may be more in the compound," he said. "They are extremely dangerous." His eyes snapped up to Maxim's. "Be careful."

7

"Do you have any idea where the tunnels could be?" Zyyr asked as Lila gathered items from the bedroom and then moved toward the kitchen to collect food for their journey.

"No," she said, shaking her head. "I told you, Idella never admitted that that story was anything more than a fairy tale. She wouldn't have mentioned the tunnels being real to me."

"And there's nowhere that you can think of that she liked a lot or that she visited often? Somewhere that could be where the tunnels are?"

Lila packed as much of the food that she had put in the kitchen of the house into her bag as she could and then turned to Zyyr.

"No," she repeated. "We rarely left the house when we were spending time together."

"Rarely," Oro said, taking a step further into the kitchen. "That means that you did. Where did you go when you did leave? Where did she take you?"

"The orchard," Lila said. "We would go into the orchard

to pick fruit. It's the same orchard that I brought you through, Zyyr. There are only trees, no tunnels."

Zyyr felt disappointment settle into his stomach. They didn't know where this place was, and the tunnels were the only way that they would be able to get there without having to spend days and possibly weeks traveling. The thought brought sudden realization to Zyyr's mind. He rushed across the house and spread the book on the table again. He sifted through the pages until he found the picture of the silver-haired creatures welcoming Idella.

"What is it, Zyyr?" Oro asked.

"What do the tunnels remind you of?" he asked.

Oro seemed to think for a moment and then stepped up to the side of the table, staring down at the book along with Zyyr.

"The tunnels to the mirrored realm," he said.

"Exactly."

"Mirrored realm?" Lila asked.

"The woman that we were telling you about with the compact, Loralia, she lived with her kind in a place under the Denynso compound. It is a mirror of the compound above it. We discovered it because of a tunnel."

"I'm sure that there are many tunnels around the planet. They used to be the most efficient way of moving around without being exposed to the elements," Lila said.

"Yes," Zyyr said, "but Loralia's kind didn't always live under the ground. Her kind, silver-haired people who use compacts to make things happen, used to live on the land that is now the Denynso compound."

"What do you mean they use compacts to make things happen?" Lila asked.

"I can't explain it," Zyyr said. "It's something that you would have to see. All I know is that it sounds exactly like what you were talking about your great-grandmother doing but on a larger scale."

"Do you think that the place that Idella visited was what is now the Denynso compound?" she asked.

Zyyr shook his head.

"No," he said. He pointed to the illustration. "This doesn't look like the compound. These plants are different and we don't have a river like this. Loralia mentioned, though, that the area that is the Denynso compound now was where they lived when they were above ground, but that then and when they moved underground they would still visit another place to gather food. She had never been, but her family would go into another place to gather fruit and other foods. It was close enough that they were able to travel there through their underground realm. None of us have seen it, though, which means that it is far enough from the compound that we have not been able to see it from the ridges."

"I don't understand what that has to do with Idella."

"What if where she visited was actually the place where the silver-haired creatures would go for food? She may have visited the actual settlement but not have included it in the book because, while beautiful, it is not like this."

"Where is the tunnel to the underground realm?" Lila asked.

"It is on a ridge in the Denynso compound," Zyyr said.

Lila made an exasperated sound.

"That is days away," she nearly shouted. "How does that help us?"

Zyyr turned to her, meeting her eyes in an effort to keep her calm.

"Because it tells me how to find the tunnels that led here."

. . .

SEVERAL MINUTES later they were walking into the orchard. Zyyr was carrying his bags as well as the bags that Lila had packed, and his eyes were locked on the ground in front of him. They walked deep into the orchard and he examined the base of every tree that they passed. He was beginning to think that his impulse might have been wrong when he noticed what he had been looking for. Lowering himself to his knees, he flattened his hand onto the patch of thick moss on the ground. It stretched a few feet from the base of the tree and felt warm beneath his palm. He looked up at Oro who stared down at him with a look in his eyes that told Zyyr that he was thinking the same thing that he was.

"Lila, did your great-grandmother come to this area of the orchard often?" Zyyr asked.

Lila looked around and then nodded.

"Yes," she said. "This tree," she flattened her hand on the tree across from the one with the moss at its base." She walked around the trunk and then looked at him. "Look," she said.

Zyyr got to his feet and went to the tree where Lila was standing. She had her hand rested on the trunk right beneath a set of initials carved deep into the trunk. *F + I.*

Positive now that his assumptions were correct, he moved back to the moss and grasped the edge with one hand. He pulled and felt resistance. Moving his hand a few inches along the edge he pulled again and felt the moss giving way beneath the pressure of the tug. Finally it rose up off of the ground, revealing a wide opening just like the ones in the orchard on the Denynso compound. He looked up at Oro and then to Lila, who stared down at the ground with widened eyes and her mouth slightly open.

"What is that?" she asked, her voice powdery as if she knew the answer to the question that she had asked but still felt as though she needed to ask it.

"It is an entrance to the tunnels," Zyyr told her. "There are several openings like this throughout the orchard in the Denynso compound. They lead down into the mirrored realm where Loralia and her kind lived."

"Idella was visiting the entrance to the tunnel," she said, sounding as though the realization was settling into her. "When she brought me here it was because she missed Finean and the other place. Why do you think that she never went back?"

"She said that the kingdom was her home."

"But she traveled back and forth before she settled here. If she loved that place so much, why did she never go back to visit?"

"Maybe she was afraid. Maybe she knew that if she continued visiting that the others would find out the secret that she wanted to keep from them. She said that people finding things out can sometimes cause more harm than good. That could be part of it."

Lila nodded. Zyyr's heart ached for his mate. He could see how hard this was for her, and there was nothing that he could do to help her. They couldn't stop now. He reached into his bag and pulled out a light stick. Pointing the illumination down into the opening, he took a breath and swung his legs over before letting go and dropping into the darkness.

For a moment he worried that there was nothing beneath him, then he felt his feet hit soft ground and he stumbled forward. Zyyr lifted his hands in front of him and caught himself on a wall a few feet ahead.

"Are you alright?" Lila called down.

Zyyr straightened and held the light stick so that he could look up and see her at the edge of the opening staring down at him.

"I'm fine," he called up. "Come down. This is it."

Oro helped Lila into the opening and Zyyr caught her, holding her close to his body as he lowered her down to the ground. He felt himself responding to her intensely in that simple movement and craved time when they could be alone together again.

Once Oro dropped to the ground, Zyyr lifted Lila so that she could move the moss back into place, covering the opening and preventing anyone else from finding it. As they started down the tunnel Zyyr's thoughts wandered to Jem and the horrific battle waged under the ground. They had thought that Ullie and the human flight attendant who had betrayed the Denynso and aided the Klimnu had been the ones to implement the technology that helped them to get down into the realm faster, but now Zyyr was realizing that this was not the case. Instead, the technology was in place in many other tunnels as well, helping those who knew of them to move around the planet undetected. The thought was unnerving, but at the same time thrilling as he felt that they were finally on the path to what Pyra had intended when they first left the compound to explore the planet.

Zyyr tried to remain aware of how far they had gone as they traveled, but after a few hours of walking he knew that they had passed through portals and were now far further from the Mikana kingdom than his awareness told him. Suddenly they came to a section of the tunnel that split off, leading in two different directions.

"Where do we go?" Lila asked.

Zyyr held up his light stick to shine the illumination down each of the tunnels. They looked identical, neither giving any indication of which would be the right option to lead them to the lush and beautiful land where Idella had found the first clues as to who she really was.

"This way," Oro said.

Zyyr turned and saw him gesturing toward one of the tunnels. He looked absolutely confident in his choice.

"Are you sure?" Zyyr asked.

Oro nodded.

"Yes. I can feel it."

Zyyr nodded and allowed Oro to guide then down the tunnel. The temperature in the tunnel was cool and the darkness surrounding them was making it difficult for him to interpret the time of day that it had gotten to in the time that they had spent below ground. They continued on for a little while longer before he realized that Lila was falling behind. Her steps had grown shorter and she seemed to be forcing her body along.

"Are you tired?" he asked, coming up behind her and wrapping an arm around her waist to support her.

She looked up at him and nodded, her long eyelashes falling heavily over her wide eyes. She was so incredibly beautiful and Zyyr felt a surge of even greater protectiveness toward her. He didn't know what they were walking in to, but he did know that no matter what, she was his greatest priority and he would do anything that it took to protect her.

"Let's rest for a few hours," Oro said. "It won't be too much longer."

"How do you know?" Lila asked as Zyyr lowered their bags to the ground and started setting up a meager camp for them.

He glanced up at Oro who was staring down the tunnel in the direction they were walking. He noticed the other warrior's hands clenching and unclenching slightly at his sides.

"I just know," Oro said, his voice taking on a tone of slight aggression that it had not held before.

Realization struck Zyyr and despite the uneasy feeling that it brought to his stomach, he couldn't help but feel the slight smile come to his lips.

8

———————

The tunnel was quiet except for the sounds of Zyyr and Lila breathing deeply from their bedrolls several feet away. Oro lay on his back on his own blanket, his hands folded behind his head as he stared up at the top of the tunnel. They had turned down the light stick so that it only let off a slight glow but his eyes had adjusted to the dimness enough that he could make out the rough earth that formed the top of the tunnel. As he stared at it he wondered about the creatures who had created it. Though they knew now that Idella and Finean had used them to travel between the settlement of the silver-haired people and the Mikana kingdom, and that there was an entrance to the tunnels in the orchard of the kingdom, that didn't mean that the Mikana had built those tunnels originally.

From the way that Lila had described it, Idella and Finean were the only ones who knew about the tunnels, and their use of them had been extremely secretive. It was possible that the technology that allowed fast and easy passage was an innovation of the Mikana but that the tunnels themselves were not widely known.

Even as Oro tried to focus on these questions rolling through his mind, his thoughts continued to wander the intense feelings that had been building within him as they traveled through the tunnels. Something within him had changed as soon as he dropped down from the orchard floor and it had only grown as they had moved further and further away from the kingdom. It was a feeling of aggression and anger, a shortness of temper that made him feel ready to lash out at either of his traveling companions at the slightest word.

This alone would not have been strange considering the tension that was building around them and the stress that was forming as they headed almost blindly into the unknown. As he traveled, however, it was the changes that came over his body that kept his mind reeling. He could feel a need rising within him, a desire that was unlike anything he had ever experienced. His body was responding to that need intensely, making his shaft so hard it nearly hurt as it pressed against the front of his pants. It was something that he would never have anticipated experiencing while on this journey, and something that he didn't know that he was prepared to face, though he, like all of the other warriors within the Denynso clan, had been waiting for it his entire life. The change that had come over him and was causing the violent temper and constant arousal could only be explained in one way. He was close to meeting his mate.

The realization that his mate was somewhere nearby was one that had completely taken him by surprise. That thought had never even crossed his mind when he left the Denynso compound for the first time in his life and started on the venture that was intended to be an exploration of the planet. Like the other warriors he had been thinking only of what they would discover along the way and what that would teach them about the planet that they called home and the other species that lived there. It would never have occurred to him to think that the woman who had been intended for him from the beginning of his life would be waiting for him somewhere along his journey.

It seemed that he had just drifted to sleep when Zyyr shook him by his boot, waking him to tell him it was time to move along. Oro stood reluctantly and packed his bag, accepting the food that Lila held out to him before starting up the tunnel again. Though they had started this exploration with Zyyr clearly leading them, the positions had shifted and now he was the one that was ahead of the other two, guiding them along the tunnels with the powerful draw within his chest pulling him in the right direction as they went.

He continued to follow this feeling as they wound their way through the tunnels. The passage that they followed seemed abandoned and forgotten, but there were times when he thought that he heard movement through the walls or saw glimmers of light deep in the tunnels that they were not following, as if there were others down in the tunnels as well. The thought was unsettling. If there were others, he had to wonder if they were aware of this area of the tunnels, and how they would respond to knowing that the three of them were now following them.

The darkness and close space was slightly disorienting and Oro didn't know how long they had been traveling or even the time of day or night that it might be when he felt an intense, almost breathtaking surge of arousal within him. All of the muscles in his body tensed and violent aggression flowed through him as though moving in his very blood. He wanted to scream, to strike out at anyone or anything that got close to him. Oro struggled to suppress the feelings, reminding himself of the turmoil that those urges had caused other Denynso who were going through this difficult phase. Though it was one of the most difficult things that he had ever tried to do, he knew that he had to hold himself back. There would be no benefit to giving into them now. It would only work to distract them from their goal and possibly prevent them from accomplishing what they had set out to do.

Instead, Oro used the intensified feelings within him to fuel him forward, allowing him to push through the exhaustion that was dragging on him and continue forward. As he walked he was aware that the ground beneath his feet was gradually leading up so that they were climbing up toward ground level. He hoped this would mean that they would not have to climb out of the tunnel through a hidden hatch the way that they had gotten in. That would eliminate the concern that they would not be able to find the exit and all of this travel would have been for nothing. As they wound their way through the tunnels, the passages took on less and less of an abandoned feeling. Soon they appeared as though they had been used within just a few years rather than having sat empty for decades.

Finally he allowed his urges to guide him around a last corner and they entered a tunnel that felt fresh and alive, as though filled with air just breathed and touched by the presence of people still within his reach. Within moments he could see a milky shimmer of light coming into the tunnel from an entrance just ahead. He paused and looked back over his shoulder to ensure that Zyyr and Lila were close to him. He had pulled ahead of them hours before, preferring to be alone with his thoughts than having to fight to control himself around them. They soon came around the corner and he saw Lila's eyes brighten as she saw the light ahead of him.

"An exit," she breathed, sounding almost as though she were reluctant to put much volume to the word for fear that acknowledging it would somehow make the exit disappear.

As soon as the thought rolled through his mind Oro felt a sense of panic come to his chest. He realized that if they were right and these were the silver-haired creatures that had been Loralia's kind before the plague that devastated them, killing all but her, it was entirely possible that what they were seeing ahead of them was not an authentic exit at all. It could simply be a reflection, mimicking the safe exit in a way that would guide intruders in the tunnel into danger rather than to their intended destination.

Lila started to pass him, and Oro held up his arm to stop her.

"What are you doing?" she asked.

"Do you believe that exit is really there?" he asked her.

"What?" Lila asked, sounding confused and exasperated.

"That exit," he said, pointing at the gap in the stone ahead of them. "Do you believe that it is really there?"

"I don't understand what you're asking me."

"Is it there?" he shouted.

Lila took a step back, cowering closer to Zyyr, but Oro didn't care about her show of fear. She nodded.

"Yes," she said. "Of course, I do."

"Zyyr," he said, turning to look at the other warrior. "How about you? Do you believe that it is there?"

Zyyr looked over Oro at the shimmer of light and then back to Oro.

"Yes," he said.

His voice sounded reluctant and almost regretful, as

though he knew exactly what Oro was thinking. Oro nodded and turned to look at the exit again.

"Well, I don't," he said.

"What does he mean?" Lila asked.

Oro ignored her and stalked toward the exit, his eyes focused directly on it.

"I don't believe that it is here. I don't believe that this is really an exit of the tunnels. I think that it was crafted and that if we tried to go through it, we would end up somewhere far worse than where we intend."

"What do you mean it was crafted?" Lila asked.

"Just like your great-grandmother used to make things happen with her compact. I think that one of their kind crafted this as a final form of protection. It's not real. It's not an exit at all, and I'll prove it to you."

Oro stared at the shimmer of light and stepped up closer to it. He told himself again that it wasn't real, that it was just like the wall in the meeting hall or the mirrored realm beneath the ground. It was an illusion, though one that could be made very real just by the belief of the person perceiving it.

"It's not real," he told himself again and reached forward with one hand.

As soon as his hand drew close to what looked like the exit, the shimmer of light disappeared and his hand came into contact with hard, warm stone. Oro could hear Lila gasp behind him and he turned to look at her.

"That is what we meant when we said Loralia could do things. She can create things just like that, but in order for it to work, the person perceiving it has to believe in it completely. If you do not fully believe that it is there, it won't be. Can you still see the exit?"

"Yes," Lila said, "but it flickered."

"It's not real, Lila," Oro told her. "You need to believe what is real, that you are looking at a solid wall of the tunnel."

He watched her take a long breath and then her eyes widened slightly.

"It's gone!" She looked frantically between Zyyr and Oro.

"How are we going to get out?" she asked, her voice now high with fear. "If that wasn't really an exit, how are we supposed to get out of these tunnels?"

"You have to believe that we will," Oro told her. "You have to really believe it. Don't just say that you do. Don't just tell yourself that you do. You have to reach inside of yourself to that place that told you that that fairy tale your great-grandmother read you was more than just a story, and believe with everything that we will find the way out. Question everything that we see and don't believe that anything is the way that you think it is."

"I think I know where it is," Lila answered softly.

"Where?" asked Zyyr, coming up to rest his hand on her back.

"You told me that what Loralia makes, like what my great-grandmother and the rest of her kind made, are reflections. If that image was created, then that means that it was reflected from somewhere."

She turned around and faced the wall opposite of where the image of the exit had been.

"Where do you think it is?" Zyyr asked.

"Here," she said, flattening her hands on the wall in front of her. "This is where the exit is. This is what will lead us to where Idella lived when she first came to this planet."

Oro felt the draw within his chest again, more powerful this time than it even had been before, and he nodded.

"Yes," he said. "That's it. That's where it is."

In an instant the wall disappeared beneath Lila's hands and the three were bathed in soft, milky light from outside. Oro stepped forward out of the tunnel and looked around. His eyes fell on the large trees and lavish plants that had been in the pictures in Idella's book. He breathed in air that was sweetly perfumed by flowers blooming among the leaves. He took another step out into the open space and suddenly heard a scream as something hit him, sending him crashing onto the ground.

9

O ro grunted as he hit the ground and felt something heavy come down on top of him. Lila continued to scream behind him and he heard Zyyr shout. The weight on top of him shifted as he heard Zyyr shouting at whatever was on top of him to get off. Oro felt a harsh blow to his head and pain radiated through his body.

"Anson!" a woman's voice said. "Stop this instant."

The weight on top of him eased and Oro was able to roll over onto his back as he gasped for breath. When he opened his eyes he saw a man standing over him, glaring down at him with a fury in his eyes that was chilling. He was not large by the standards of the Denynso, but was certainly larger than the Mikana men or the human men he had encountered. It was not his size, however, that took Oro aback. It was the huge translucent grey wings that stretched on either side of him.

The man who Oro assumed was Anson stepped back away from him and he felt the primal need within him swell as a new light appeared just before a stunningly beautiful woman stepped up beside Anson. She had the soft, glimmering light around her that Loralia did and wings like delicate pink glass. She reached a pale, graceful hand toward him.

"Let me help you," she said softly.

Her voice was like music and everything within Oro seemed to come alive as he place his hand in hers and climbed to his feet.

"Thank you," he said.

"Who are you?" Anson demanded in a gruff voice. "Why are you intruding here?"

"Hush now, Anson," the woman said in a softly scolding tone. "They aren't intruding. Can't you see," she stepped forward and Oro saw her take Lila by both hands and lead her carefully forward, "she is no stranger."

The woman ran her fingers through Lila's hair, bringing some of the strands forward as if to show off the silver streaks to the winged man. Anson's stiff stance relaxed slightly as he looked at Lila's hair, but he had the same suspicion in his eyes when he turned his gaze back to Oro.

"Who are they?" he asked. "Why are they with her?"

"Why don't you ask her," the woman said, "and allow her to tell you for herself? What is your name?" she asked, looking to Lila.

"Lila."

"Hello, Lila. My name is Ariella. This is my brother, Anson. I apologize for his less than hospitable greeting."

"It's alright," Lila said. She gestured toward Oro. "This is Oro." She stepped back slightly and turned to reach for Zyyr. "And this is Zyyr, my mate."

Oro noticed Ariella's eyebrows lift slightly at those words, but she continued to smile at them, the expression making Oro feel weak and somewhat out of control.

"You are welcome here," Ariella said. "Come with me. I'm sure you are hungry and tired after your long journey. You will stay in my home with me."

"Ariella," Anson protested, but the winged woman turned her brother and lifted a hand to silence him.

"Not another word, Anson. They are our guests. You will not offend the memories of our friends and family."

The words fell painfully on Oro. He didn't know what she meant, but the emotion in that message felt heavy. Anson nodded once and turned away from them. Ariella followed and the three fell into step behind her. The dress that Ariella wore fastened around her neck and then swung low over her hips, and Oro watched her graceful back as she walked, admiring the smooth expanse of her skin and the incredible wings that stretched from between her shoulder blades. Anson and Ariella led them through plants that looked richly green even in the moonlight that fell on them toward a series of gently sloping hills in the distance. As they got closer Oro noticed that there were doors in the hills and realized that these were their homes.

Anson ducked into one of the doors and closed it tightly behind him without saying another word to them. Ariella watched him and then opened another door, gesturing for them to enter.

"Please come inside."

They did as she asked and Oro found himself stepping into a home that was as unexpected as Ariella herself. Everything within the home seemed to be fashioned out of leaves and carefully bound branches with only small bits of fabric added in. There was no cut wood in the house, but rather elements of the world around them that had been thoughtfully salvaged and creatively utilized.

Ariella gestured for them to sit and Oro took his place

on a chair that rocked gently on curved legs. He used his feet to increase the rocking, allowing the motion to soothe him. Zyyr and Lila sat together on a small sofa.

"I have to apologize for my brother," she said. "He takes his position as guard very seriously."

"It's alright," Oro said. "Protecting you is the most important thing that he could do."

He felt heat creep across his cheeks as Ariella turned to look at him, her eyes registering slight surprise at his words. He could feel Zyyr looking at him now and he knew that the other warrior already knew what he was going through.

"Thank you," Ariella said softly. "Now, I am sure that you have a reason for coming here, but I think it is best that you eat and rest. There will be plenty of time tomorrow for you to tell me what it is that I can do for you."

The three agreed and Ariella walked out of the room, returning a few moments later with a tray of food that she settled onto the table in the center of the room. She left again and returned with another tray that she set alongside the first. She left a third time and returned with tall glasses and a curved pitcher. Zyyr reached for the food first and Oro followed suit, picking up a piece of something that he didn't recognize and looking at it. Though it didn't look like anything that he had ever eaten, knowing that Ariella's hands had made it made him immediately want to eat it.

They ate until they were satiated and then Oro sat back in his chair, feeling the exhaustion really settle into him now that they had arrived at their destination and his belly was full.

"If you have all had enough, I can show you to your rooms. There are baths in each and you are welcome to wash if you would like."

They followed her deeper into the home and Ariella

pointed out a room for Zyyr and Lila first. When they had thanked her and closed the door behind them, she gestured at him to follow her further down the hallway. She brought him to a door and opened it, stepping back so that he could enter. The room as far larger than he anticipated and in contrast to the wood and leaves of the first room, this one was light and soft, delicate like Ariella. A soft-looking bed piled with white blankets looked incredibly inviting, but he also felt the dirt and sweat of their journey sticking to his skin and knew that he should take her up on her offer of bathing before settling in for the night.

"Thank you, Ariella," he said, his voice coming out slightly powdery.

"Are you alright? Anson didn't hurt you badly, did he?"

Oro shook his head, somewhat embarrassed by the scuffle, but also enjoying the fact that she was concerned about him.

"No," he told her, "I'm fine. He mostly just knocked the wind out of me. It was a shock more than anything."

"Good," she said. She paused and their eyes met for a brief moment that Oro could feel coursing through him. "Sleep well."

"I will."

He stepped back and she closed the door. Oro waited a few moments and then crossed the room to the sunken bath in the far corner, disrobing as he went. He groaned as he let his pants fall to his ankles, finally releasing the pressure on his engorged cock. Being close to Ariella had only increased his arousal and now Oro felt like he couldn't handle it if he got any harder.

The water that poured from the faucet was the perfect temperature and Oro sank into it blissfully, letting the heat release the tension in his muscles and rinse away the reminders of the tunnels that clung to his skin. He filled his palm with soap from one of the bottles lining the edge of the tub and ran it back through his hair, then went through the process of washing his body. He submerged himself completely to rinse and when he came out of the water he was startled to see Ariella standing just steps from the edge of the tub.

"You are a Denynso warrior," she said simply.

Oro nodded.

"I am," he confirmed.

"I suspected as much when I saw you, but I knew when Lila described Zyyr as her mate."

"Yes," Oro said, not sure how else to respond.

"My mother warned me about Denynso when I was young," she said, stepping closer to the tub.

"She did?" Oro asked.

Ariella nodded, a soft smile coming to her lips. There was something fragile and innocent about her that made his desire for her even more intense and Oro fought to resist the urge to reach for her.

"She told me that the Denynso men are powerful in many ways and are fearsome in battle. Even more, perhaps, than our own warriors. When they meet their mate, however, they are insatiable until they have her and irresistible when they want her."

Oro found himself walking up to the edge of the tub as she approached and lowered herself to her knees. She reached out and ran her hand through his hair then gently touched the back of his head as if checking to make sure that he was not more severely injured than he had admitted.

"That's true," he said.

"Do you have a mate, Oro?" Ariella asked, her fingers wandering to the plane of his jaw.

"I think so," he said quietly, tilting into her touch.

"You think so?" she asked.

Her voice sounded nervous and he ached to comfort her, to show her that she was safer now than she had ever been in her life. He shook his head.

"I know," he whispered.

Oro tilted his mouth up to hers and Ariella met it. Her lips were soft and sweet against his and Oro felt like a flame had ignited within his belly. He reached up to tuck his hand around the back of her head and drew her closer to deepen their kiss. He guided her gently with the tip of his tongue and Ariella complied, parting her lips so that he could explore her mouth. When the kiss ended Ariella looked breathless and flushed, her eyes slumbering but also bright as though she couldn't decide what to do with the new feelings that she was experiencing. She dipped her hand down into the water beside Oro and filled her palm, lifting it up and tipping it so that the warm water slid down his chest. She repeated the gesture and he watched her eyes as they traveled with the drops along his skin. Her gaze stopped and she bit down on her bottom lip, color rising even higher on her cheeks. Oro looked down to see what had caught her attention.

He hadn't noticed that coming closer to the edge of the water had caused him to rise up out of it slightly and now the tip of his hardened cock sat above the water. Oro brought his hand to it, running his palm across the head and then stroking down over the shaft. He heard Ariella moan softly and he looked at her, waiting until she met his eyes to take her hand and guide it forward to replace his. The movement caused her to lean forward over the edge of the tub and he took advantage of the position to kiss her again and then reach around to the back of her neck to release the tie of her dress. The fabric fell away from her body and he ran his flattened palm down her back, letting the tips of his fingers touch the juncture of her back and her wings, but not venturing onto the wings themselves.

Ariella seemed timid about touching him, but continued to gaze into the water with fascination and desire. Oro wrapped his hand around hers, tightening her grip on his shaft and beginning to guide her in stroking him. She gasped softly and Oro moaned at the intoxicating combination of her hand on him and the sweet sound coming from her lips. After a few moments he felt her pulling her hand away. He was briefly nervous that he had moved too fast with her and that she was going to leave, but then he saw her stand and push the dress down her hips, allowing it to fall away completely.

She wore nothing under the dress so now she stood in front of him with her lush body bare and waiting for him. He had never seen anything as incredible as her, the swells of her hips full and sultry, her breasts gently sloped with taut pink nipples, and a tiny waist that seemed to accent all of her soft, enticing curves. Ariella looked at him with a nervous, questioning look in her eyes and he let out a long exhalation.

"You are beautiful," he said.

She smiled and reached for him, both delicate hands extending out to welcome him to her. Oro climbed out of the water and took her hands, allowing her to bring him forward toward her until their bodies just touched. Their marked height difference made it so that her mouth was just beneath the center of his belly and he drew in a breath as she ran her lips softly across his skin. He ran his fingertips along her arms, delighting in the velvetiness of her skin. The tips of her wings fluttered slightly and a moment later she rose off of the ground, coming up until she was able to look him in the eye. The impact was mesmerizing and Oro felt that he couldn't control himself any longer.

Grasping Ariella by the waist he leaned forward and captured her mouth with his, kissing her more deeply and insistently than before. He moved one hand to wrap tightly around her waist and slid the other down the curve of her belly until it dipped between her thighs. She cried out against his mouth as his fingers found her already hot, wet folds and began to explore them. Oro held her closer as she writhed against him, slipping one of his fingers within her and using the pad of his thumb to massage the taut pearl that his attention was easing forward. As her tight, untouched body started to relax, Oro slipped in another finger, taking his time to allow her body to take it in.

He kissed along her neck until his mouth reached the soft place beneath her ear.

"Are you ready for me?" he whispered.

She was nearly sobbing with the pleasure that he was already giving her and she nodded, tucking her head down onto his shoulder.

"Are you sure?" he asked.

"Yes," Ariella responded, touching a kiss to his neck. "Yes, I'm ready."

Oro slowly withdrew his fingers from her body and returned his hands to her waist so that he could carefully position her over his hips. He settled her at the tip of his erection and eased her forward, slowly sinking into her. Suddenly, unexpectedly, Ariella's head fell back and she cried out. The glow around her intensified for a moment and Oro felt her already tight walls squeezing around him as her climax drew him in deeper. He moaned, rolling his hips slightly to meet each of the delectable spasms as she rode the waves of the orgasm that had hit her so intensely as soon as he was fully inside her.

As the contractions slowed Oro carried her over to the bed and turned so that he could sit on the mattress. He lowered himself back, positioning her so that she was straddling his hips. Her body was even wetter now and relaxed by the climax, allowing him to press deeper within her. He gripped her hips and guided them into a rocking motion that let her grind against him without their bodies parting. Ariella looked uncertain and slightly taken aback by her own sexual response, drawing her arms up to cover her breasts and looking away.

"Don't cover yourself," Oro said, reaching up to take her arms and ease them away from her body. "You are so beautiful. I want to see you. All of you."

He led her hands down to his stomach so that she flattened her palms against him. Her long hair had tumbled down from the knot that had held it to her head and now hung wildly around her. Oro tucked one hand around her cheek and Ariella turned her face to touch a kiss to his palm. As if empowered by the kiss, she started to follow the guidance of his hand still on her hip, falling into a rhythm that threatened to send him into oblivion within seconds.

In an effort to prolong the almost overwhelming pleasure and remain as close to his new mate as he could, Oro sat up, pulling Ariella in close so that she cuddled into his lap. She responded by wrapping her legs around his hips and crushing her breasts to his chest. This position allowed them to stare into each other's eyes, elevating the intense emotions that were taking over Oro's mind and heart. Their skin moved across each other slickly with water and sweat, and he savored the feeling of her breasts rising and falling against his body.

He could no longer resist. He brought one hand up and ran it gingerly down the edge of one of her wings. It fluttered and he groaned slightly. He touched it again, amazed by the texture of it beneath his fingertips. As he stroked her wing with one hand, Oro slipped the other between their bodies so that he could mimic the touch on her most sensitive peak. She rocked against his hand, her eyes closing and tiny cries spilling from her lips. Oro lifted his hips, pounding into her in rhythm with the grind of her pelvis. He quickened the pace of his fingers on her body and she screamed out again, grasping his shoulders with both hands as she released into a cascade of new contractions.

Oro let out a growl and thrust into her with an almost frenzied pace. Within seconds he felt himself spiral out of control and plunged as deeply into her as he could. Letting out a gasping cry he gave himself over into his own orgasm, spilling into her with each pulse. As their bodies cooled he let himself tip back again, bringing Ariella down with him so that she lay across his chest, her head rested just above his heartbeat. He kissed her hair and watched as her wings slowly folded down and tucked against her body as she drifted to sleep in his arms.

10

Rain finished packing all of the supplies that she could into her bags and turned to watch Lynx secure his closed. She didn't know how long they were going to be away or what they would encounter along the way, so they needed to bring everything possible with them. They started out of the house, but were almost immediately stopped by another of the former Nyx 23 crew.

"What are you doing?" Jonah asked, starting intently into Rain's eyes.

"I can't tell you," she said, trying to step around the man to continue out of the settlement.

"Rain, you know something that you aren't telling me."

Jonah had been one of her dearest friends while traveling on the Nyx 23 craft and then on the settlement, and in that moment she realized that in the time since they had been released from the lock put on them by the Covra she had spent almost no time with him. The thought made her feel guilty and regretful, but she knew that she had to press forward. What she and Lynx had discovered was important and she needed to find out more as quickly as she could.

"I'm sorry, Jonah," she said, fighting off the tears that were starting to form in her eyes at the thought of leaving her friend behind again.

"I can help you."

"I'm not going to put you in danger."

Jonah stopped walking but Rain continued.

"What about our project?"

Rain stopped in her tracks and whirled around to face Jonah.

"What project?" Lynx asked. "What is he talking about?"

Rain couldn't answer her mate. Instead she rushed back to Jonah, her heart fluttering wildly in her chest.

"Our project," she breathed. "I don't know how I could have forgotten it."

"You seem to have forgotten a lot," Jonah said, his voice sounding slightly bitter as he watched Lynx walk up behind them.

"Please, Jonah, don't be that way."

"What project is he talking about?" Lynx asked again.

"Do you think that it's still there?" Rain asked.

She didn't want to get her hopes up thinking that the project that had not been touched in over 100 years was still intact where they had left it.

"I know it is," Jonah said.

Hope swelled in Rain's chest. Jonah turned and started toward the edge of the settlement where they had constructed a small, simple structure they hoped would function as their lab while they were on Uoria. At first a few of the others had been excited by the idea and used the space to perform simple experiments and run tests on the plants and soil of the planet, trying to glean as much information about it as they could. Rain knew that it was their way of keeping their hope alive. As long as they gathered this information they could believe that one day they would be able to share it with the rest of the scientific community back on Earth. Before too long, those who had joined them stopped coming and the lab was left completely to Rain and Jonah. Though Rain had seen it as a failure of the motivation and scientific devotion of the other members of the crew, Jonah was excited by the departure.

It was his enthusiasm for having his career-long dream of having his own dedicated lab coming true, no matter what the circumstances, that spurred them into starting their project. Neither had ever told anyone else about it and in the tragic, hectic weeks leading up to the final Covra attack they had abandoned it, choosing instead to focus their energies on the direct attacks and protecting themselves. Now she wondered if it was even possible for the makeshift lab to still be there, much less their only partially completed project.

She rushed through the settlement, trying to suppress the hope that was building in her but also not able to contain her excitement. Ahead of her rose the building that they had constructed largely out of the outer shell of the original ship. Though worn and covered with encroaching plants, the lab was still there, still standing. Jonah stepped up to the door and yanked on it. The door groaned but didn't move. He tried again but it still wouldn't move.

"Excuse me," Lynx said from behind them.

Rain and Jonah stepped out of the way and Lynx planted a perfectly aimed kick directly in the middle of the door, causing it to crash into the building.

"Thank you," Rain said, climbing onto the balls of her feet to kiss her mate. "I appreciate it."

"Any time," Lynx replied. "Now will you tell me what project you were talking about?"

"Just a minute," Rain said.

Lynx gave a grunt of frustration, but Rain ignored it. She looked around the space, letting the memories of that building wash over her. Jonah was already rushing toward a door on the far wall that led to the smaller room. This had been their private space and where they had conceived and begun to build their project. She rushed after him, relieved to see that he was able to open that door with greater ease. She didn't want Lynx to have to break down this door as well and risk damaging whatever was left inside.

The door opened and Jonah hesitated to go in.

"What if it isn't there anymore?" he asked.

Rain stepped up beside him and nudged him with her shoulder.

"And what if it is?" she asked. "What if this is our chance to finish it?"

"Would it help you?" Jonah asked.

Rain nodded.

"Yes. More than you know."

"I don't know anything. You won't tell me. You never kept anything from me."

Rain felt her heart squeeze. The truth was that she had been holding things back from him since the crash. She knew that no matter how much she had tried to avoid it, tried to protect others from what she knew, the time had come to tell Jonah what had really happened.

"You're right," she said. "I'm sorry. There are things that I should have told you from the very beginning that I didn't, and that is my fault. But I'm willing to tell you about them now."

Jonah immediately settled onto one of the chairs in the room, crossing his legs and propping his chin in his hand in the position that he always used to tell people that he was listening to them. If what she had to tell him had not been so serious, she would have laughed at the pose. Now, though, it only made her more afraid of how he was going to react. She settled onto another of the chairs so that she could look at him and gave a deep sigh.

"Etan killed himself," she said, deciding the best way to handle the situation was simply to throw herself into it and tell Jonah everything right out.

"What?" Jonah asked, sitting up and letting his hand lower down so his arm fell across his legs.

Rain nodded.

"When the ship lost power and started to crash, I went to the control room to see if he knew what was happening. The ship crashed before I could get there. When I got into the room I found him. He was barely warm to the touch already."

"He had been dead for some time," Jonah said.

Rain nodded again.

"I didn't know what happened, so I never told anybody. Even you."

"So how do you know that he killed himself?" Jonah asked. "Something else might have happened. One of the Valdician weapons could have –"

"No, Jonah," Rain said, cutting him off as his emotions sent his voice higher and faster.

"But Etan was so devoted to the project. He dedicated his life to being a captain."

"That's exactly what he did," Rain agreed. "This team, this mission, was everything to him. Being the captain and doing right by the crew was the most important thing in his entire life."

"So why would he kill himself?"

Rain lowered the bag on her shoulder to the ground and

dug through it until she found the journal that they had taken from Etan's quarters. She handed it over to Jonah. She knew now that he was a part of this, as he likely should have been from the beginning. He had been on the perimeter of everything that had happened from the moment that the Denynso had succeeded in starting to awaken the members of the settlement after being frozen in place by the Covra for more than a century. It was time now that she brought him in and benefitted from not only his brilliance and incredible understanding of science and technology, but from the emotions and memories that he had within him. So much of what she and Lynx, as well as the others, were learning was discovered simply through memory and intuition. Though much of Jonah's memories were shared with her, she knew that he had many of his own that may give them greater insight into what had actually happened to them and to the others affected by the Validicians and the Covra.

Jonah finished reading the journal entries that Rain pointed out to him and looked up at her, shaking his head.

"How could he do that to us?" he asked. "He abandoned us."

"He didn't see it as abandoning," Rain said. "To him, we were all going to die within just a short time anyway. It was his way of continuing to be our captain, our leader."

"If he killed himself before the crash, what good would our project do now?"

Rain handed him the map and pointed out the strange symbol.

"We need to go there," she said. "Lynx and I believe that that is where we were originally supposed to crash and something got off course somehow. We need to know what is there and why that was where we were supposed to end up."

"That's pretty far away," Jonah said. "If we can complete our project it could make that journey much easier for you."

"What project?" Lynx asked again and Rain could hear the frustration and growing anger in his voice.

She got up and walked to the center of the room where she had Jonah had propped several sheets of scrap metal years before. She took hold of one of the pieces and pushed it aside, then repeated the gesture with a few more pieces. Finally she turned to her mate and held out a hand in presentation.

"This project."

TBC

(To be continued in book X...)

www.ingramcontent.com/pod-product-compliance
Lightning Source LLC
Chambersburg PA
CBHW032040180726
48284CB00008B/2681